TANDEM

D1164376

Assassination Brigade

The meeting drew to a close, and both the Soviet chairman and the US security adviser were standing to shake hands.

Then one of the men in the Soviet chairman's own party – later I learned that he was the Russian ambassador – took a step toward the Communist chairman. He was holding a grenade that he had pulled from his pocket. The man unpinned the grenade and dropped it on the plush carpet directly at the Russian leader's feet.

In the split second of frozen horror that followed not a sound could be heard in the room. I could see the pure terror on the face of the Soviet chairman as he gazed down in helpless fascination at the lethal activated grenade lying at the tips of his shoes.

At that moment, with every person in the room paralyzed, the Russian ambassador – the man who had dropped the unpinned grenade – flung himself on top of the explosive. There was a muffled blast; the grenade's deadly power was smothered by the man's body. He was blown apart, his head torn from his torso. . . .

Assassination Brigade

Nick Carter

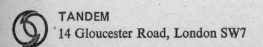
TANDEM
14 Gloucester Road, London SW7

Originally published in the United States by
Universal-Award House, Inc., 1973

Published by Universal-Tandem Publishing Co. Ltd, 1974

'Nick Carter' is a registered trademark of the
Condé Nast Publications Inc.

Dedicated to
The Men of the Secret Services
of the
United States of America

Made and printed in Great Britain by
Hunt Barnard Printing Ltd., Aylesbury, Bucks.

ASSASSINATION BRIGADE

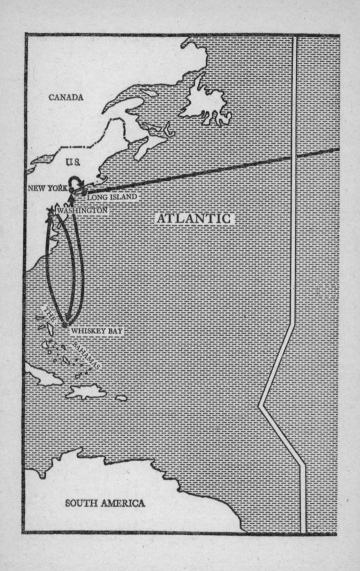

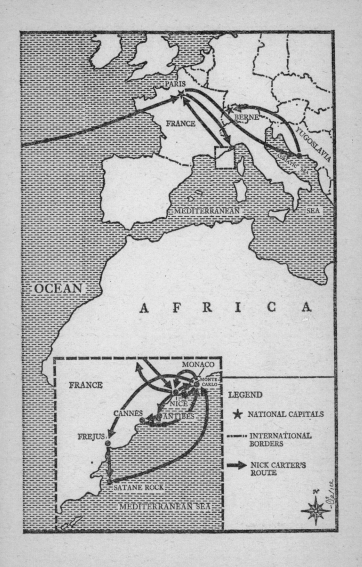

One

I knew when the phone rang in the gray, pre-dawn hours that it could only be one person on the other end of the line—Hawk, my boss at AXE.

The phone was on a night table on the opposite side of the bed, so I had to crawl over Maria Von Alder, asleep beside me, to reach it. Maria stirred in her sleep, drawing up one leg slightly so that her sheer pink nightie rode up above her hips, as I scooped up the receiver.

"You're needed back here immediately," Hawk said as soon as he had identified my voice. His words were clipped and urgent. "There's been a new development in that deal we're working on. Be ready to leave in thirty minutes."

"In thirty minutes?" I asked. "How? You seem to have forgotten where I am."

I was on Whiskey Cay, a tiny island off the Bahamas, where Hawk himself had sent me on assignment. I would have to arrange for a boat to pick me up and take me to one of the larger islands so I could catch a plane back to the States.

Hawk was impatient with my answer. "Be ready

7

to leave in thirty minutes," he repeated, his voice icy. "Mr. James is providing your transportation."

I nodded without speaking. "Mr. James" was the AXE code-name for the President of the United States.

"Good," Hawk said, as if he had seen me nod. "A boat will pick you up at the main dock of Whiskey Cay in precisely twenty-seven minutes." He hung up. As I put down the receiver, I saw that Maria had opened her eyes and was watching me.

"That was my office in New York," I told her. "I'm afraid I have to go back. The company's sending a boat."

Maria thought I was a millionaire named Tony Dawes, the cover I was using on my present AXE assignment. Even if she had heard my conversation with Hawk, she still wouldn't have any reason to doubt my cover.

But she made a face, her ripe, red lips pouting. "Do you *have* to go back today?"

"Yes, I'm afraid so," I said cheerfully as I started to swing out of bed. "And not just today, but right now. I've just about got time to dress before the boat gets here."

But before I could get out of bed, Maria reached up and playfully tugged at my arm, pulling me toward her.

"You don't have to be in that much of a hurry," she said huskily.

There was no doubt about it. Maria Von Alder was a beautiful creature, a long-legged, shapely blonde with a superbly molded, golden body and full, smooth breasts, their pink tips thrust hard against the bodice of her transparent gown. She was looking at my body, and she could see what the sight of her was doing to me. She slithered down the bed on her back, her hips slightly up-raised, offering her silken body to me, like a loving cup waiting to be filled.

With all the willpower I could muster, I whispered, "There'll be other times." I brushed her cheek with my lips and took off for the shower.

I couldn't complain that the past five days on Whiskey Cay hadn't been enjoyable. The island was a pleasure playground for the very rich. There were luxuries everywhere you looked—the sea-going yachts, scrubbed clean, riding at anchor on the sparkling blue waters; the acres of expensive, landscaped lawns, blazing with flame-bright flowers, stretching away to the sea; the clusters of palatial villas, vividly colored, as if they had been drawn with a child's crayons, cresting high above the Atlantic Ocean. I had been enjoying everything, including Maria Von Alder, for the past five days.

But my visit to Whiskey Cay had still been frustrating; I was there on business, and I was no closer to a solution of my current assignment than

I had been the day Hawk first briefed me at AXE headquarters in Washington.

Hawk had opened the conversation with an uncharacteristic monologue about the dangers of this particular mission, the impossible odds, the vital importance of success.

I had shot him a look out of the corner of my eye, thinking, so what else is new? I'd half-expected to see those wrinkle lines around his thin lips break into a smile. It wasn't often that Hawk, a reserved New Englander, tried to be humorous. But I saw that these lines around his mouth and piercing eyes only deepened, and I knew he meant it.

He shuffled some papers on his desk and frowned. "We were just informed—it's top secret, of course—that six hours ago the Prime Minister of England was threatened with assassination by his life-long friend, a fellow member of Parliament. The two men were at the Prime Minister's country house when the friend suddenly produced a rifle, aimed it at the Prime Minister, and then, quite inexplicably, turned the rifle on himself and blew his own brains out. There was no one else present at the time, so we can give out a fake story to the public. But the real implications of the incident are frightful."

I nodded. This was more bizarre than I'd expected, even after Hawk's lead-in speech.

"The official British version is going to describe

it as an accident," Hawk continued. "A misfire while the friend was examining the rifle. Of course, it will not be mentioned that the weapon was first turned on the Prime Minister."

"Are you planning to lend me to the English to help with the investigation?"

Hawk shook his head. "The problem is closer to home. There have been reports of similiar occurrences in China, France, Japan, and Germany. In each instance the would-be assassin had the power to kill his victim but instead killed himself.

"You can imagine what effect these reports have had on the President. He could easily be the next target. And he's not about to wait until a member of this assassination squad reaches the White House, even if the killer eventually murders only himself. Our job this time is to search out and destroy—preventive action."

"Do we have any leads?"

"Not much," Hawk admitted. He lit one of his cheap cigars and puffed in silence for a minute. "I have all the files of the investigations from the various intelligence agencies in each of the countries and those of Interpol as well. Want to know what they've found?"

He ticked the facts off on his fingers. "One, all the dead assassins were overweight. Two, all were obsessive about their excess poundage and spent considerable time trying to get rid of it. Three— three of them were close to the Von Alder sisters."

I raised an eyebrow. "Terrific. I'm looking for fat men on a diet who like pretty girls. You're not exactly making this easy."

"I know," Hawk said. "I'm sorry." From the way he said it, I almost believed him. But then he turned crisply businesslike again.

"We start with the Von Alder sisters—that is, you do. They're the only real clue we've got."

The Von Alder girls were a little bizarre themselves. Maria, Helga, and Elsa—identical blonde triplets, well known to any newspaper reader or television viewer. They were in their twenties and beautiful. They had come to the United States from Germany after World War II with their mother, Ursula. They specialized in millionaire husbands and lovers, who'd made them wealthy with gifts of homes scattered around the globe, yachts, jewels, even private jets.

Thinking it over, I decided that getting close to the Von Alders was probably one of the most pleasant ways I'd ever started on an assignment.

It had been simple enough for AXE to supply me with a cover—Tony Dawes, wealthy businessman who had inherited a prosperous export-import business with headquarters in New York. Soon, with Hawk pulling the right strings behind the scenes, I'd been invited to a number of the same parties as the Von Alder girls. Once I met the sisters, it was reasonably easy, with lavish displays of gifts and attention, to become a part of their social set.

Maria was the first Von Alder I "investigated." I'd taken her to Whiskey Cay, where we spent five blissful days in luxury. But I had uncovered no further leads by the morning Hawk ordered me back to the United States.

Two

A little less than twenty minutes after Hawk's call, I headed down to Whiskey Cay's main dock. Maria Von Alder went with me, clinging to my arm. The boat was already waiting there—a forty-foot cruiser, most of its paint peeling and rusted, its twin diesel engines idling. There were four men on deck.

One of the men, who was wearing a faded baseball cap, called out, "We're all set to shove off, Mr. Dawes."

"Be right with you," I answered. I turned to say goodbye to Maria, and she gave me a long, demanding kiss.

"Remember, Dumplink," she said—all the Von Alder sisters called their men "Dumplink"—"stay away from those sisters of mine or I scratch the eyes out."

"Mine or theirs?" I asked.

"All the eyes," she said.

She gave me another quick kiss, and I vaulted onto the deck of the cruiser. The man in the faded baseball cap immediately cast off. As the cruiser's

powerful twin diesels throbbed to life, I saw a
second boat sweeping in toward the dock. It turned
suddenly and headed toward my cruiser, which
was making swiftly toward the open sea, its prow
knifing through the water, its bow making a
rooster-tail of spray. Soon Maria Von Alder, still
standing at the end of the dock, had shrunk to the
size of a doll and then disappeared completely.
Within minutes the island itself had vanished from
view.

Suddenly I realized that the other boat was
pursuing us. The familiar chill ran down my spine.
Somebody had made a bad mistake—could it have
been me?

I tried to figure it out, and quickly. Either the
other boat was an enemy craft, trying to get at
me, or I had let myself be picked up by the wrong
boat and the other vessel was the one Hawk had
sent to Whiskey Cay. Before I had a chance to
work on it some more, the man in the baseball
cap told me what I wanted to know.

"You will please do nothing foolish, Mr. Dawes,"
he said. He shoved back a length of tarpaulin on
the deck and snatched up a sawed-off shotgun
that had been lying beneath it. The barrel was
leveled at my chest.

At least he didn't know my real name. But I still
couldn't explain how he knew I'd be waiting at
the dock on Whiskey Cay for a boat. Either some-

one had been listening in on Hawk's call or Maria Von Alder had given me away.

There was a shout from the man at the wheel of the cruiser, and the boat veered to starboard with a sudden lurch that almost knocked us all off our feet. Then we saw what the trouble was— a sinister silver object streaking through the water almost directly across our bow. The boat pursuing us had fired a torpedo, but the missile just missed us and went hurtling out to sea.

But that brief moment, with all hands on board the cruiser thrown off balance, gave me the opportunity I needed to pull out Wilhelmina, my modified Luger with a three-inch barrel. While I was with Maria on Whiskey Cay, I had kept it hidden in a secret compartment in my luggage. But before I left our suite that morning, while Maria was in another room, I had prudently slipped it into my crotch holster, which I wore inside my trousers so that I could reach the gun by opening my fly.

While the man wielding the shotgun was still sprawled against the railing, I crouched, unzipped, and yanked out the Luger. I could see the bug-eyed amazement on his face when the Luger appeared out of my fly. He yelled and swung the shotgun's muzzle up, his finger tightening on the trigger. We fired simultaneously. Wilhelmina's 9mm slug closed the gap between us a scant half-second faster. The bullet blew the man's face away and sent him crashing through the railing and into the sea, his shotgun pellet blasting into the bulkhead behind me.

I moved quickly, grabbing a life jacket with one hand and stuffing the Luger back into its holster with the other. Then I jumped the railing into the sea. I guessed that the men on the second boat had been signaling me to try to get out of the boat when they fired the torpedo and that they were watching me through binoculars.

Despite the heat of the day, the water was shockingly cold when I hit and went under. Still clutching the life jacket, I bobbed up almost at once and began paddling away from the cruiser toward the second boat, now speeding toward me. Over my shoulder I could see the cruiser start to swing around in pursuit.

The cruiser was still midway in its turn when the approaching boat fired another torpedo. The sea missile whizzed past me, only about five yards away, and this time struck the cruiser midship. There was one hell of an explosion, and I was buffeted by violent shock waves that radiated through the water like electric current skipping across an exposed live wire. The cruiser blew apart, sending up a giant geyser of water, debris, and bodies.

Seconds later, the pursuing boat had pulled alongside, and helping hands were lifting me aboard. Once on deck, I saw that this boat was an exact replica of the cruiser that had just been destroyed; even to the flaking and rusted paint and the number of men aboard. But this time one of the men flashed a card with a United States seal and the President's signature.

"Sorry about the inconvenience," the man said shortly. "We were late getting to the dock at Whiskey Cay. Somebody had performed a little piece of sabotage on our generators to delay us. When we saw the other boat pull away with you, we guessed what had happened."

"Thanks," I smiled. "You did a nice job of recovery."

A real professional, he didn't bother to acknowledge. Instead, he said, "Perhaps you'd like to change into some dry clothes before we reach our destination. You'll find an outfit below in the cabin."

I went below and changed into fresh denims, sweat shirt, shoes, and socks. They weren't exactly Saville Row attire, but they were clean and dry. My rescuers hadn't asked me any questions or volunteered any information. They were probably CIA, but I still didn't have any idea how they planned to get me back to the mainland with the speed that Hawk had in mind.

When I went above again, the same man who had spoken to me earlier told me that we should be reaching our transfer point in approximately six minutes.

I nodded, but I still didn't know what he was talking about. We'd been out of sight of Whiskey Cay for awhile, and from what I knew about this area of the Atlantic, there was no land for miles to the west except the U.S. All I could see were mountainous swells of blue sea on every side.

Exactly five minutes and fifty seconds later we came within sight of a U.S. Navy aircraft carrier, and the man on deck with me said, "Here we are —right on the button."

A score of jets, wings folded, were perched on the carrier like dark birds catching a brief rest before resuming flight. Some crewmen dropped a rope ladder as our boat pulled up alongside. I shook hands with my rescuers and then scrambled up the ladder. The cruiser had pulled away and was almost out of sight in the rolling sea before I had reached the deck.

The ship's captain met me at the top of the ladder, snapped a salute, which I returned, and quickly hustled me to a jet that was waiting on the flight deck. The engines of the A-4 Skyhawk were already whining impatiently, anxious to be airborne. I shook hands with the pilot, a young redhead, put on flight clothes, and crawled into the rear cockpit. The pilot gave me a "thumbs up" signal, and we catapulted down the deck of the carrier and into the sky with breathtaking speed. When the President of the United States acted as your personal travel agent, the accommodations were strickly first class. . . .

Three

The flight back to the States was swift and un-eventful. Our destination was New York's JFK airport, and we landed there on a special runway that had been cleared for us. After the sun and clear skies of Whiskey Cay, I wasn't prepared for the blustery, biting January cold of New York.

Hawk was waiting at the end of the landing strip in a long, dark limousine. As soon as I had transferred from the jet to the car, the red-headed pilot waved his hand, turned his aircraft around, and took off for the carrier. There were two men in the front of the limousine—the chauffeur and, I guessed, another AXE agent. I knew we must be facing a serious crisis, since Hawk almost never revealed the identity of one agent to another. Hawk tapped on the glass partition that separated us from the men in front, and the limousine rolled across the airport.

"Well, N3," Hawk said, staring at the window, "I assume you have no new information to report."

"I'm afraid not, sir," I said, but I did tell him about the duplicate cruiser at Whiskey Cay and my rescue. I added, "Of course there's no way to prove how they got the information. Maria Von Alder may not be involved at all."

"H'mm," was Hawk's only response.

We rode in silence for several seconds before Hawk turned and said glumly, "The chairman of the Russian Communist party is due to arrive here at JFK in approximately six minutes. He'll be meeting with some of our people in a hush-hush session at the U.N. before he flies back tomorrow. We've been given responsibility for his safety while he's here. That's why I needed you back so urgently."

It was my turn to mutter, "H'mm."

The limousine had slowed down, and now it stopped beside one of the airport runways, where a large crowd of people and cars were waiting. Hawk leaned forward and pointed to a giant Turbo-jet that was descending from the leaden skies. "Our visitor is right on time," he remarked, glancing at the pocket watch he wore on a chain strung across his vest.

As soon as the Russian plane stopped on the runway, airport personnel quickly rolled steps up to the cabin door, and the Soviet party chairman emerged. He was followed from the huge plane by several other Russian officials, and at the front of the steps the whole group was immediately surrounded by police and security officers—both Russian and American—and escorted to a waiting line of cars. When the procession, led by a phalanx of New York motorcycle police, drove off, our limousine was directly behind the Soviet chairman's car. Soon we were entering the gates of the United Nations, with its long stately row of flags flapping briskly in the chilling wind.

Once inside the building, the whole group was quickly whisked into one of the private security-council chambers. It was a spacious, windowless room with seats arranged in tiers, like an amphitheatre for spectators, with a podium in the center, where the Soviet chairman and his party and the United States security adviser and his assistants took their places. Hawk and the other AXE agent and I had seats in the first row of the tiers, next to the Russian security police, who had accompanied the Soviet leader from Moscow. Behind us were city, state, and federal law-enforcement agents. The meeting was, of course, closed to the public.

The two men communicated through an interpreter, who translated in whispers from one to the other so that nothing that was said could be heard where we sat. It was like watching a play in pantomime and trying to guess what the actors were saying from their gestures.

At first it appeared that both men were angry and suspicious. There was a lot of frowning, scowling, and fist-banging. Soon the anger gave way to puzzlement, and then I could see that the two men were becoming more friendly. Apparently they were beginning to realize that neither country was behind the bizarre incidents.

Soon after, the meeting began to draw to a close, and both the Soviet chairman and the U.S. security adviser were standing to shake hands.

Then one of the men in the Soviet chairman's own party—later I learned that he was the Russian ambassador—took a step toward the Communist chairman. He was holding a grenade that he had pulled from his pocket. The man unpinned the grenade and dropped it on the plush carpet directly at the Russian leader's feet.

In the split second of frozen horror that followed not a sound could be heard in the room. I could see the pure terror on the face of the Soviet chairman as he gazed down in helpless fascination at the lethal, activated grenade lying at the tips of his shoes. In an instinctive reaction I drew my Luger, Wilhelmina, from the holster, but Hawk grabbed my arm. Actually, as he had been quicker than I to see there was nothing I could do. A bullet would only explode the grenade faster. There wasn't even time for the Russian leader to move from the spot.

At that moment, with every person in the room paralyzed, the Russian ambassador—the man who had dropped the unpinned grenade—flung himself on top of the explosive. There was a muffled blast; the grenade's deadly power was smothered by the man's body. His body was blown apart, his head torn from his torso.

The repercussions of the explosion staggered the Soviet chairman and the others on the podium, but otherwise they were unharmed. Hawk and I immediately hustled the Russian and American delegations from the room to the waiting limousine outside. Arrangements were hastily made for the U.S. security adviser and his staff to return to Washington and for the Russian party to go to the Soviet Embassy and remain there until they left for Moscow.

Meanwhile, emergency police ambulances and the N.Y.P.D. bomb squad began to arrive at the U.N. with a contingent of newspaper reporters and photographers. The private security council chamber had been blocked off by U.N. police, but Hawk and I were allowed back inside where the sheeted remains of the Russian ambassador were being loaded onto a stretcher. Already, members of the Russian security police and American agents were preparing to trace the recent movements of the ambassador.

A call was placed to the White House, and the President was informed of the affair. Before that conversation ended, Hawk was called to the phone to talk with the President. When he came back, the AXE chief's face was gray.

"That was a near disaster," he said, shaking his head. "The President has advised me that we will receive a full report on the Soviet ambassador's movements as soon as the investigations turn anything up. But we already know one thing."

"What's that?"

"Just two nights ago," Hawk said, "the Soviet ambassador was a guest at a party thrown by Helga Von Alder and her mother at Helga's Park Avenue apartment."

"Are you sure?" I asked, startled.

Hawk nodded toward the other AXE agent who had accompanied us in the limousine from Kennedy. "Agent Z1 was at the party. Since I knew it was impossible for you to keep an eye on all the Von Alder women at once, I've been using him on the case. I want you two to get together at once so he can give you the details about that evening. Afterward, I want you to work on Helga Von Alder. And. . . ."

"Yes sir?" I asked.

"I'm sure I don't have to remind you about the urgency of your mission. There must be a link somewhere between this business and the Von Alders. Find it, no matter what it takes."

Four

Hawk went on alone to the New York AXE office, leaving Z1 and me to talk together. After spending most of the day in the jet flying from Whiskey Cay and in the car driving from JFK, I felt I needed a workout at the gym. I suggested to Z1 that we go to the athletic club for a game of handball while we talked.

Neither of us, of course, knew the other's real name. Z1 himself was about my age, a couple of inches shorter and several pounds heavier, with straw-colored hair and a fair complexion. As soon as we had changed into gym clothes and started our game, I saw that he was a worthy handball adversary. He had a clumsy, flat-footed lope on the court, but he hit the ball with murderous power so that it bounced around like a richocheting bullet and kept me moving.

"That party the other night was quite a bash," he began, and I detected a faint southern accent in his voice, a sort of middle-southern-states accent. "Those Von Alders sure know how to entertain. There were a couple of actors, the Russian ambassador, two British authors, that pop artist who paints nothing but pictures of jock straps, and a dozen other people I never did get to meet."

"Did any of them seem particularly cozy with the ambassador?" I asked, taking a whack at the ball and, in a lucky shot, driving it hard into Z1's midsection, making it impossible for him to return the shot.

"Whew!" he mumbled, straightening up with an effort, his face beaded with sweat. Then, in answer to my question, he said: "It appeared to me that all the guests there were pretty chummy with one another. Like they were all charter members of some exclusive club. You know what I mean?"

I nodded. "But was Helga or her mother, Ursula, ever alone with the ambassador for any length of time during the evening?" I asked, racing back and forth across the court. I didn't know what kind of information I was expecting to get from him, but any kind of lead or link between the dead ambassador and one or another of the Von Alders would help.

"No," Z1 answered, doing his own share of running. "Actually, the Russian spent most of the time talking with that artist and finally wound up the evening buying two paintings the fellow had brought along. It struck me as the worst kind of capitalistic decadence for the Communist to pay good money for paintings of jock straps."

I had a sudden, wild idea. "What would you

think if I asked AXE to arrange an autopsy on the dead Russian's brain?"

"An autopsy?" Z1 exclaimed, swinging around and looking at me. "What could an examination of his brain prove?"

"It's just a hunch," I said. "I can't get it out of my mind how weird the whole situation is. Not just what happened today, but all the previous killings—or I should say suicides. These men have formed the strangest assassination squad I've ever seen. Maybe they'd been drugged first, or hypnotized, or brainwashed. Somebody had to have gotten to them to make them behave in such an identically irrational way. There's got to be an explanation. Maybe an autopsy would provide some answers, help us understand the reasons behind the case."

"I suppose it's worth trying." Z1 shrugged.

"Hawk wants me to move in on Helga right away," I told him. "As soon as we finish the game, I'll call her and try to make a date for tonight. I guess you'd better report back to Hawk at headquarters. Be sure and tell him that I want to get an autopsy done on the Russian."

"Sure thing," he said, missing a shot and losing the game to me.

After we had showered and dressed, we went to a bar and had a couple of chilled martinis, and I called Helga Von Alder from a phone booth.

"Dumplink!" she squealed delightedly as soon

as she heard my voice. "You're back. That dumb sister of mine let you get away. Will I see you tonight?"

"Exactly what I had in mind," I told her. "I'll pick you up about eight."

When I had completed the call, Agent Z1 and I parted company. I headed for the luxurious Sutton Place apartment AXE had leased for me—or rather for "Tony Dawes."

One of the advantages of undercover work for AXE was that the organization spared no expense in creating a fool-proof disguise for its agents. The apartment of "Tony Dawes" was a good example. It was a smart, elegant bachelor pad, complete with all the accessories of seduction that such a man would provide for himself. Soundproofed from outside, high enough to give a view of the city—and privacy—and engineered with all the latest electronic equipment from intimate lighting to quadrophonic sound throughout. My only requests had been a small gym and a sauna. I spent the remaining hours of the day working out on the punching bag and parallel bars and finished with a sauna bath. It was seven thirty-five when I set out in my dinner jacket to call on Helga Von Alder.

Helga's apartment was a penthouse on Park Avenue in the eighties, in a regal building that looked more like a private club than a residence. I had expected her to be alone, but when I arrived,

I saw that Ursula was there with a gray-haired gentleman, whose face looked vaguely familiar although his name momentarily eluded me.

"But Dumplink," Helga greeted me, planting the usual open-mouthed Von Alder kiss on my lips and pulling me inside, "say hello to Ursie"—the Von Alder daughters called their mother Ursie—"and her escort, Byron Timmons." I recognized the man then as one of the country's oil tycoons. Ursula Von Alder also gave me a kiss on the lips that was far from maternal, and Timmons shook my hand stiffly.

"Ursie and Byron were just leaving," Helga added, smiling cherubically.

Byron Timmons muttered, "Ah, yes," and began to help Ursula into her mink coat.

"We were talking about the terrible accident poor Vladimir Kolchak had," Helga said. "You heard it on the news?"

"No," I said. "I'm afraid not."

"He was killed at the United Nations this afternoon," Helga said sadly, "some kind of boiler explosion."

"Terrible," I said, wondering if Hawk had concocted the "boiler explosion" for the press all by himself.

"Poor Vladdy," Helga said, "he was always so full of life. I'll miss him."

"You knew him?" I asked.

"Oh yes," Helga answered. "He was an old friend

of Ursie's. He was here at the house, at a party, just two nights ago."

"We'll all miss him," Ursula repeated, kissing Helga on the cheek, brushing my lips with hers, and heading for the door. Byron Timmons followed after giving me another stiff handshake.

As soon as Helga closed the door behind the departing couple, she collapsed into my arms with stifled giggles, whispering, "Oh, Dumplink, Byron Timmons is awful angry at me—and you. When I made the date with you this afternoon, I had completely forgotten I was supposed to go to the theater with him tonight. When I remembered, I had to do some frantic rearranging and call in Ursie for a substitute. I told Byron you were an old friend I hadn't seen in years and you were in town only for the evening."

"I knew he wasn't exactly happy about something. Now I understand."

Helga pulled away, shaking her head. "Sometimes I can be so naughty. But I wanted to be with you."

"I'm pleased," I told her, "and flattered. Now where would you like me to take you?"

"It's such a nasty night out," Helga said softly, "I thought maybe you'd just rather stay here and be cozy. If you don't mind making do with something simple like champagne and cavier. I'm afraid that's all we have in the house, and it's the servants' night off."

"I can't think of a nicer way to spend the evening."

She had surprised me. She was dressed in a skin-tight, white evening gown, her blonde hair carefully coiffed, a diamond necklace around her throat with matching diamond pendants swinging from her earlobes. She was ready for a night on the town. But then I realized that the Von Alder women probably dressed like that just for an evening of lounging around the house.

Helga turned on some music and turned down the lights. Soon she brought out the champagne and caviar, and we sat side by side on a leopard-skin chaise in front of floor-to-ceiling windows where we watched the city lights and snowy darkness.

"You know, Tony," Helga said softly, turning toward me as we both sipped the chilled champagne, "you're not like the other men I've known in my life. I can usually figure them out pretty easily, figure out what they want from a woman. With you I'm not so sure, though I haven't known you for very long. And that's a challenge. I find it exciting, and I think all the other Von Alder women, including Ursie, do, too." She sat up straight suddenly. "Did you enjoy yourself with Maria?"

I nodded truthfully. "She's lovely. But then, you all are. After all, you're identical triplets."

"Not completely identical." I could see her smile

in the semidarkness. She put her champagne glass down and slid over on the chaise, nestling her body next to mine. I could feel the warmth of her flesh through her gown. The exotic scent of her perfume stirred my loins. I slipped a finger under the strap of her gown, then paused.

"Helga," I said.

"H'mm?"

"This fellow, Kolchak or Vladdy, as you called him—did you see much of him recently?"

She misunderstood my question. "You don't have to be jealous of him, Dumplink." She wiggled her body closer to mine so our thighs touched.

"No, but I'm curious," I persisted. "Did he visit you or your family often in the past few weeks?"

She shrugged, still pressed against me. "Vladdy was one of those people who was always around, or always seemed to be around, among my friends. You noticed him when he was there, you didn't miss him when he was absent." She stirred impatiently. "But that's the past—this is the present. The present is always more important."

I knew that was all she was going to say. Perhaps she wanted to conceal something, or perhaps she truly had nothing more to say about Kolchak. At any rate, I felt I had fulfilled the responsibilities of my assignment for the moment.

Now I had a responsibility to myself not to let this opportunity slip between my fingers. I used those fingers to ease the strap of Helga's dress. She slid both straps down her arms, and the soft, white cloth fell to her waist.

She wore no bra. As she leaned back, her full, shapely breasts tilted up, pink-tipped nipples erect. She squirmed forward to meet my face so that my mouth was filled with one and then another of the melonlike mounds. Her body quivered violently as I caressed her nipples with the tip of my tongue until finally, with a shuddering gasp, she took my head between her two hands and lifted my lips to hers. As we kissed, she ran the fingers of one hand down the length of my thigh until they encountered the evidence of my arousal. Her hand lingered there momentarily.

"Lovely, Dumplink, lovely," she whispered breathlessly, moving her lips to my ear.

I lifted her and carried her across the livingroom, through the foyer, and into the bedroom. An enormous round bed stood in the center of the room. I lowered her onto it, and she peeled off her dress, hose, and lace bikini panties. Lying on the satin sheets, she reached impatient hands up to help me strip off my clothes.

I could feel my blood race as my eyes devoured her spectacular body. She was an exact duplicate of her sister Maria, from the perfectly-formed, thrusting breasts and gently curving hips to the small golden triangle at the center of her body. She pulled me to her, and when our bodies touched, she turned her head to one side and said softly, "Look, Dumplink, everywhere you turn you see us make love."

Until then I hadn't noticed that three walls of the room, at the head of the bed and on both sides, were completely mirrored. As Helga's body coiled and uncoiled with mine, like some perfectly programmed yet delicate instrument of sensuality, the mirrors reflected the sensuous movements as if we were in the midst of a huge orgy where we were the entire group of participants.

And I found, as Helga had told me, that she and her sister Maria weren't completely identical. There was a big difference in the way they made love. Both women made love with infinite imagination and tremendous, open pleasure. But there the similarity ended. While Maria had been silent and intense, her movements exquisitely subtle, Helga was wild and abandoned, her hands, hips, and mouth constantly exploring my body, exchanging pleasurable sensations for each one she received. Her whole being was continually writhing, quivering, and stimulating me to greater and greater heights of ecstasy. It was as if—and the mirrored walls heightened the effect—I was making love to a dozen different women, each with a different approach and reaction. Finally, she gave a high cry of pure pleasure and fell back on the bed.

After a moment she leaned over me. "I make you happy?" she asked, covering my face with kisses.

"Yes," I said. "Yes, you make me happy."

"I'm happy, too," she said. "You are the man I thought you were."

I pulled her gently toward me so she lay on top of me, our bodies pressed together from head to toe. We lay motionless, neither of us speaking. After a moment she gave me the small gasp of surprise I was expecting.

"Shh," I whispered to her.

She was silent again, but not for long. "Oh!" she cried. "Oh! Oh, Dumplink! OH!" Her body shook convulsively again until, with a long, low moan of rapture, she rolled over on her back and shut her eyes.

My regular programs of body and mind exercises had come in handy once again, enabling me to give Helga a final gift of pleasure she hadn't expected.

Five

Helga opened her eyes and smiled softly up at me as I bent my head over hers. "It was lovely, lovely, lovely," she whispered. She rolled over and climbed out of bed. "You rest, Dumplink," she said, kissing me and leaving the room.

In a moment she returned with a bottle of champagne and two glasses. She filled one of the glasses and handed it to me. "This," she said, "will keep you occupied while I take a shower." She kissed me again and went into the bathroom, humming happily. As I stretched out luxuriously on the bed, I could hear her running the shower.

I took a sip of the chilled Dom Perignon. Outside the wind had risen. The fourth wall of the room had drapes across it, and I knew that behind the drapes were doors to the penthouse's garden that ran around all four sides of the apartment. Behind the door something was banging. I set my glass of champagne down next to the bed, pulled on my trousers, and went over to the door. When I pulled a section of the drapes aside, I saw

38

that one of the doors was ajar and swinging in the wind. I pulled the door shut and latched it.

I was halfway back across the room when that infallible sixth sense, a subconscious warning of impending danger, sent me its message. Without knowing why, I instinctively flung both hands up in front of my throat. I'd acted none too soon. At the same instant, a thin wire noose was being tossed over my head and settled around my shoulders. The wire, which would have been embedded in my throat, was, instead, cutting deep into the flesh of my out-flung hands.

There was a heavy grunt from my assailant and a savage jerk on the noose. I ducked and rammed backwards with my shoulder. I still couldn't see who was behind me, but in that sudden lunge, I did catch a fleeting glimpse of two struggling images in Helga's wall of mirrors. I looked again and saw myself and the man behind me reflected there. The man was Z1!

His face was contorted with the effort of his assault, but there could be no mistaking his identity. It was the same man I'd played handball with at the athletic club that afternoon.

It was impossible to try to figure out why he was trying to kill me now. All I could do was defend myself. And it was an eerie, unsettling sensation to be watching someone trying to murder me in the very same mirrors where only a short time before I had seen myself and Helga intensely enjoying sex.

He still hadn't noticed the mirrored wall and didn't know I was watching him in it. He started to raise his leg to jam his knee in my back. I kicked out savagely with my left foot and caught him in the kneecap, smashing it. He gasped in pain and started to fall, pulling me down with him. I tried to squirm out of the wire noose, twisting my head around as I fell. He held doggedly to the noose, still trying to strangle me. I could see his face clearly now. His eyes were glazed—as if he were hypnotized or drugged.

Up until now I had hoped to be able to defend myself without killing him. But I saw that was impossible. I drove the rigid edge of my right hand into the base of his throat with a lethal karate chop. The blow was hard and clean. His neck snapped, and he was dead, probably without ever knowing what killed him. His body sagged to the floor, the head twisted grotesquely to one side. I pulled myself up and stood there, straddling his body.

I could hear the shower going in the bathroom. The deep pile carpeting on the bedroom floor had muffled the sounds of our struggle. It seemed obvious to me then that Helga Von Alder had lured me to the bedroom, knowing that Agent Z1 was going to make an attempt on my life afterward. As good as she had been with me in bed, I could never forget that she and her sisters were all experienced actresses.

On the other hand, I reminded myself, there was still the possibility that she was innocent. Z1 had known I was seeing Helga this evening and could have tailed me to the apartment. If, as I now suspected, he had orders to kill me, he could have slipped into the room from the terrace while Helga and I had been making love, and she wouldn't have known any more about it than I did.

If that was true, I couldn't let Helga appear from her shower and find a man I had killed lying on her rug. There could be no explanation that would satisfy her without blowing my cover. If I did that, the only lead that AXE had on the case, the Von Alders, would be worthless. There was only one thing I could do—turn the body over to Hawk, who had all the facilities at his command for discreetly disposing of it.

I bent down, hoisted the corpse up by the armpits, dragged him across the room and through the terrace doors, and dumped him outside. Then I hurried to the bedside phone to call Hawk. We had to talk without a scrambler.

"This is serious business," I said as soon as he answered. Speaking tersely, I filled him in on exactly what had happened, improvising a code as I went along. I concluded by saying, "My friend and I will be leaving here shortly. Can you handle the mopping up operation?"

Hawk understood. "Leave the arrangements to me," he said, "But do drop in and see me later tonight."

"I plan to," I answered and cut the conversation short when I heard Helga turn off the shower in the bath.

A few minutes later Helga came into the room, wearing a sheer black negligee that revealed every superb detail of her body. I was again stretched out on the big bed, sipping champagne from my glass. Fortunately, the death of Agent Z1 had been bloodless, and there was nothing in the room to indicate the struggle that had occurred there only moments before. If Helga had been in on the plot and had returned expecting to find me a corpse, she gave no indication of it. Instead, she cuddled up on the bed beside me while I poured her a glass of champagne.

"*A amore*," she said, touching my glass with hers.

"*A amore*," I agreed.

After we had drunk, I swung my legs off the bed, and said, "Come on Dumpling, I'm going to take you out to dinner. Man does not live by *amore* alone. At least, not this man."

The restaurant we chose was a small, dimly lit French place not far from Helga's apartment. It was still snowing outside but the restaurant was warm and cheery, and the service and food were superb. But I really wasn't hungry, since all through the meal, I kept visualizing the grisly scene that would be taking place at Helga's apartment as Hawk had the body of the dead AXE agent removed.

Helga didn't appear to notice my preoccupation, and she ate heartily, chattering vivaciously throughout the dinner. Once she made a mock pout, the same gesture Maria had made when I left her on Whiskey Cay, and said, "Dumplink, let's take a weekend trip somewhere, so we can be alone. You went off with Maria. Now it's my turn."

The kind of joking competition that existed among the girls amused me. "What did you have in mind?" I asked.

She made a vague motion in the air with her hand. "Mexico. Spain, perhaps. The south of France. After all, the jet is just sitting idly in the hanger. We might as well make use of it." She suggested this as casually as if she were talking about a taxi ride across town. And I could see that she was serious.

"We'll see," I said, keeping my options open since I didn't yet know what kinds of complications there were going to be from the death of the AXE agent.

Helga nodded and then surprised me by suddenly turning serious. It was a mood I never expected from any of the giddy Von Alders.

"I'll tell you something, Tony," she whispered,

her fingers intertwined with mine as we sipped our cognac. "I get vibrations from you, vibrations of great strength. It's what I've spent all my life looking for in a man. The gentleness of a caring lover and the strength of a man of authority. Sometimes you find one thing or the other. But both—never! That's very good." She frowned and said slowly, "Once I tried to explain what I was looking for to a man I know. He was gentle but not strong, and he said I felt the way I did because I had never known my own father. He said I was looking for a lover and a father-figure all in one. Do you believe that?"

I shook my head. "I never speculate about things like that, reasons for feeling. The feelings themselves are what count."

"I think so, too," she agreed. "But I do think about my father sometimes, and I know Maria and Elsa do, too, although we never speak of him."

"And you don't remember him at all?" I asked.

"No. Only what Ursie has told us. He was killed in Berlin during one of the Allied bombing raids in World War II. My sisters and I were very small then, and it was only a miracle that Ursie got us out alive."

She smiled and brightened up again. "But life has been good since then," she said.

Later, when I took Helga back to her apartment, I stopped in long enough to make sure Hawk had removed the body from the terrace. Of course he had attended to the matter. As I left Helga, she reminded me again that she wanted us to take a weekend trip together. I promised to let her know. Then I went downstairs and took a taxi to AXE headquarters.

Six

AXE's New York office was on the Lower West Side of the city in a warehouse in the dock area. The cab driver wasn't too happy when he heard the address. I guess he thought I was going to mug him en route, because I heard him sigh with relief when we pulled up in front of the place. I over-tipped him and got out. As I started across the sidewalk, he leaned out the window and asked, "You sure this is the place you want, buddy?"

I waved him away. His feelings were understandable. The whole waterfront area was dark and deserted. The building that housed AXE headquarters was blacked out except for one lighted room in the front of the building. What the cab driver couldn't know was that all the other dark windows in the building were painted over to conceal the bustling activity that went on inside twenty-four hours a day and that men with powerful infrared telescopes observed the street outside constantly. Actually, the cabbie couldn't have been safer anywhere in the city than right there, outside the most powerful counterintelligence agency in the world.

The night security man on duty in the lighted front office, which looked like an ordinary warehouse office, pressed a buzzer under his desk, and I passed through an iron door to a manned elevator. The sentries with their telescopes in the upstairs windows had already cleared me with both men while I was still approaching the building.

"Hawk left orders to take you to the basement as soon as you came in," the elevator operator said. The car descended.

The basement—that meant Hawk was waiting for me in the agency's morgue. Like most of the world's supersecret intelligence organizations, AXE had to have its own morgue on the premises to handle those corpses that couldn't be turned over to the police right away. Most of the bodies, however, were eventually placed in the hands of local law-enforcement officials after the way had been cleared so there would be no embarrassing questions asked.

I found Hawk standing beside the sheeted body of Z1. The AXE medical examiner, Dr. Christopher, was with him.

Hawk nodded to me and the medical examiner, whom we called Dr. Tom, said, "I ran a preliminary autopsy, Nick. It agrees with what you told us. His death was caused by a broken neck."

"Did you find anything else?" I asked.

Dr. Tom shook his head. "Nothing so far. Why?"

Instead of answering him, I spoke to Hawk. "Did Agent Z1 report back to you today with my suggestion that we try to get an autopsy done on the brain of Ambassador Kolchak?"

"No, he didn't," Hawk said. "He came back here to headquarters and told me that you had made contact with Helga Von Alder. I didn't see him after that. There was no mention of an autopsy. Is that important?"

"It could be," I said slowly. "It might supply us with a possible motive for his attack on me."

Hawk frowned. "I don't follow you."

I knew it was safe to talk in front of Dr. Tom, who had top-level security clearance on all AXE activities. "Well, when he jumped me in Helga's apartment, he appeared to be dazed—like someone who was not in control of himself—yet his physical actions were perfectly coordinated."

"You mean," Hawk interrupted, "you think he was one of the assassination brigade? Much as I dislike the thought that one of our own agents could be under the influence of this—this power or whatever it is, I agree."

"But that wouldn't necessarily explain why he would try to kill me," I resumed, "unless I had said or done something that was threatening whatever it is we're fighting. The only thing I can think of was my suggestion for an autopsy. Since he didn't pass the suggestion on to you but did try to kill me, it would seem that was the connection."

"What exactly did you think an examination of the ambassador's brain would show?" Dr. Tom asked.

"I don't know," I admitted. "But we have been speculating that the men involved in these incidents were brainwashed in some way. So the autopsy on the Russian was a stab at proving the brainwashing theory. Maybe we'll find nothing, but then we've got nothing to lose by trying it."

"Yes, I see," Dr. Tom said. He looked down at the corpse lying on the AXE morgue slab. He glanced at Hawk. "How about it, Chief?"

Hawk hesitated for only a fraction of a second. "Go ahead," he said, nodding.

Dr. Tom pulled the sheet up over the frozen features. "It'll take me a couple of days to do the job," he said thoughtfully, "I'll send you a report as soon as I have the results."

Hawk and I left the morgue in silence and rode the elevator up to the second floor of the building. That floor was the nerve center of the New York headquarters. A staff of more than fifty people worked there twenty-four hours a day at teletypes, radios, and closed circuit television sets that communicated with the offices of the world's police forces. The corridor that led to Hawk's office ran alongside the big room. There were one-way glass windows on the walls so that those in the corridor could see into the room but those in the room couldn't see them. This arrangement prevented other AXE personnel from observing the secret agents who reported to Hawk's office.

Once we were in Hawk's office, the chief of AXE settled wearily into his desk chair, rummaged through his pockets until he found a chewed-up cigar, and stuck it, unlit, in his mouth.

"I must confess, Nick," he said, "this case has me worried. What's your opinion about the Von Alders?"

"It's hard to say," I replied, choosing my words carefully. "As far as I have been able to determine, they're exactly what they appear to be on the surface. But it's hard to discount the fact that every time there's a new development in the case, they're somehow connected."

"Speaking of new developments," Hawk cut in, "I haven't had a chance to tell you about Monte Carlo. We just got the word tonight from Interpol."

"Monte Carlo?" I asked.

"Yes. There's a run on the casino there. A man named Tregor, a Belgian, is breaking the bank. Tregor's brother-in-law had tried to stab the Chancellor of Germany a few weeks ago, then plunged the knife into his own throat instead. We have nothing on Tregor, but you'd better go and check him out anyway.

"The casino management has temporarily

stopped the play," said Hawk. "But they've agreed to resume it in twenty-four hours. I'd like you to be there when the casino reopens, but I don't want you to be out of touch with the Von Alders. Can you manage both?"

"It's no problem," I told him. "Earlier this evening Helga pleaded with me to take a trip with her to Mexico. She said we could use her private jet."

"And you think she'd settle for Monte Carlo?" Hawk laughed. "You must put a lot into your work."

"It does have its rewards."

"I can well imagine," he answered, waving me out of his office in dismissal.

Seven

It was early, a little before 8 A.M., the next morning, when I phoned Helga's apartment. I knew that she wouldn't be up that early, but I couldn't put off calling her any longer if we were going to fly to Monte Carlo that day.

The voice that answered was drowsy with sleep. "Hello. Hello?"

"Helga," I said, "this is Tony Dawes."

"Who?" she asked, still half asleep. "Hello?"

"My God," I said, laughing, "don't tell me you've forgotten me so soon after last night. It's Tony."

"Ah—Tony, Dumplink," the answer was now full of life.

"The reason I called you so early was that I'd like to take you up on that invitation for a little trip—just the two of us. But instead of Spain or France or Mexico, let's make it Monte Carlo. How does that sound?"

"Divine," she said. "When do you want to go?"

"Right now," I told her, "this morning, as soon as possible. You did say the jet was ready."

"Of course," she said. "But why Monte Carlo?"

I'd already decided to give her the real reason for choosing Monte Carlo. Television, radio, and newspapers were running the story that morning about the run on the casino.

"You probably haven't heard the news," I said. "There's a big run on the bank at the casino. Last night the management suspended play for twenty-four hours. I'd like to be there when it starts again."

I had figured it was just the kind of thing that would appeal to a Von Alder. I knew I'd guessed right when I heard her delighted squeal.

"Let's go," she exclaimed without hesitation. "How soon can you be ready to take off? Do you want me to pick you up for the drive to Long Island?"

The Von Alders kept their jet at their Long Island estate on the North Shore. I'd visited the estate a couple of times since I'd met the family. So, since I knew where it was, I told her I'd meet her there in two hours.

I reported to Hawk and then worked out briefly in the small gym at my apartment before dressing and packing my bag. Hawk sent a car and driver to take me out to Long Island, and when we got there, I found Helga waiting and the plane ready on the Von Alder's private landing strip.

Less than two hours after I'd phoned Helga, we were airborne on the Lear jet and flying over the Atlantic. Helga and I sat in seats in the rear of the spacious cabin, which had all the comforts —lounge chairs, sofa, bar, even a crystal chandelier—of a comfortable livingroom.

It was a perfect day for flying; the sky was blue and cloudless from horizon to horizon, a welcome change from the overcast weather of the previous night. The sea beneath us was like an unruffled blue carpet.

Helga took me forward to the cockpit to meet the pilot, Captain Dirk Aubrey, and the copilot, Douglas Roberts. Aubrey was a tall, heavyset fellow with a pencil-slim black moustache. Roberts was a slim younger man—probably in his early twenties—with light-colored hair and a freckled moon face.

"She's right on course," Aubrey said, nodding toward the instrument panel, "and the weather's clear straight into Orly, where we'll refuel."

For the next several hours, Helga and I amused ourselves with a movie that she showed by simply pressing a couple of buttons and later, with a game of backgammon. Helga seemed much more subdued than she'd been the evening before, but she was still good company, and the time passed swiftly.

We must have been less than fifty miles off the coast of France when, without warning, the plane abruptly plunged with its nose down toward the sea. Helga screamed. Everything in the cabin that wasn't nailed down—including Helga and me—skidded over the canted floor of the cabin and slammed hard against the closed door of the cockpit.

Helga was still screaming while I tried to twist around on my side to push the door of the cockpit open. It was locked. I yanked out Wilhelmina, my Luger, from my shoulder holster and blasted the lock off. The door swung open, exposing the cockpit that was now below me.

As I looked into the cockpit, I could see that Captain Aubrey was still at the controls, but his posture appeared to be frozen. Copilot Roberts was sprawled on the floor, either dead or unconscious. The plane was still plummeting toward the ocean.

I yelled at Aubrey, who turned his head briefly to look up at me. Then he turned back to the controls, both hands clenching the wheel. Looking at his face, I recognized the same blank expression I had observed on the face of the AXE agent when he had tried to kill me in Helga's apartment. His eyes were glazed as if he were hypnotized or drugged.

Until that moment, I had been hanging onto the side of the cockpit door with my fingers. Now I released my grip and came hurtling forward into the cockpit. I reached for the pilot at the controls. Somehow I managed to hook one arm around his neck and pry him partially loose from the wheel, but he still clung stubbornly to the controls until I yanked at him with all of my strength and threw him backward into the rear cabin.

The plane continued its drop toward the sea.

I fell into the pilot's seat and pulled back hard on the wheel. A great shudder ran through the jet from nose to tail, but then slowly the nose began to come up. I continued pulling back on the wheel, straining every muscle in my body in my effort to defeat the pull of gravity. Finally, the plane leveled off—only a few feet from the Atlantic. It was lucky I'd put in enough flying time in jets to be able to handle that plane, but it had still been a near catastrophe.

During the next few minutes I was busy checking the instruments while the jet skimmed evenly along the surface of the ocean. Everything seemed to be working, so I shoved the wheel forward, and we began to climb again. Then Helga screamed my name from the rear cabin.

I turned just in time to see Aubrey coming at me with a wrench. While I steadied the wheel with one hand, I whipped out Wilhelmina again with the other and shot him in the right shoulder. He staggered backwards and fell, letting the wrench slip from his numb fingers. As I tried to hold the jet in a climb, I glanced back at the pilot. He had pulled himself to his feet again, but was reeling back into the rear cabin. I could see

Helga in the background, huddled up in a corner of the cabin. I still held Wilhelmina in my hand, but I didn't want to shoot again unless Aubrey made a move toward either Helga or me.

He didn't. Instead, he staggered drunkenly toward the cabin door, which he managed to shove open despite the tremendous pressure on it. There was no way to stop him except to shoot—and if I missed, I would endanger the whole plane. Aubrey hung briefly in the open doorway and then tumbled out head first. I swung the plane up and around so that the door slammed shut. Beneath the starboard wing, I could see Aubrey's body falling almost in slow motion, his arms and legs spread apart, until he hit the water and disappeared beneath the choppy surface.

Helga joined me in the cockpit while I focused my attention on flying the jet. She tried to revive Roberts, the copilot, who was still lying unconscious on the floor. It took her a long time to bring him around, but eventually he mumbled, sat up groggily, and looked around. He was shaking his head. "What happened? What's going on?"

His behavior confirmed my suspicion that he had been drugged. When he had recovered enough to speak coherently, he told me that the last thing he remembered was drinking a cup of coffee that Aubrey had handed to him. He was still too dazed to ask about the missing captain, so I didn't tell him anything about Aubrey's fate. I would concoct some kind of explanation later.

By that time, I had radioed the control tower at Orly, which we were now approaching, and we had been cleared for landing. A little later we touched down, and I brought the jet to a standstill. I couldn't say I wasn't relieved.

As we left the plane, Helga looked at me with puzzlement in her eyes. "What happened back there?"

I shook my head. "Hard to say. Looks like your captain froze to the controls and went berserk with fear when the plane started to fall. He was probably half-mad when he attacked me and then jumped out. Roberts, the copilot, must have passed out from the pull of gravity. Those things aren't uncommon in flying. But let me do the talking to the authorities so we don't get caught up in a lot of red tape."

There was no way to tell if she had really accepted my explanation, but she didn't press me further.

When we reached the airport terminal building—accompanied by Roberts, who was still shaky on his feet—I located the head of Orly's security police and asked him to send me an AXE agent, a fellow I knew as Dummlier, and the local chief of Interpol. When both men arrived, I told them exactly what had happened, indicating that I suspected the incident was tied in with my assignment. I stressed that it was urgent for Helga and me to continue to Monte Carlo immediately.

"Let me take care of this," the man from Interpol said when I had finished. "There will be no trouble. Perhaps your associate here," he turned to Dummlier, "can locate a trustworthy pilot and copilot to fly you on to your destination."

Dummlier nodded, and the meeting ended. In less than an hour Helga and I were on our way to Nice, the closest landing field to Monte Carlo. We had two Americans—probably part of the French AXE staff or the CIA—to pilot the jet. Dummlier had made arrangements to return Roberts to the States, and Helga herself had reassured him that he would continue in her employ and would be paid while he was recuperating from his unfortunate experience. As far as I could determine, my explanation—that Roberts had suffered a blackout—had been accepted by both Helga and the authorities.

The flight to Nice was without incident. We landed in late afternoon, and Helga and I took a limousine to the Hotel de Paris, near the casino in Monte Carlo. Helga had arranged to have the limousine waiting to meet our plane and had reserved adjoining suites at the hotel as well. We were lucky that Helga was well known; we were guaranteed rooms even though Monte Carlo was packed with curious tourists from all over the world. The streets were swarming with sightseers, giving the town an intoxicating carnival air, and there wasn't an empty hotel room to be had.

As we drove through the streets of Monte Carlo, with the Mediterranean shimmering like dark, rich wine in the late-afternoon shadows, I was reminded of the legendary story of the beginning of Monaco in the year 303. According to the legend, a Corsican maiden, Devote, was punished by the governor of Corsica when it was discovered that she was a Christian. The governor sentenced the girl to be bound and dragged by horses over rough ground and then to be stretched on a rack until she was dead. The instant she died, a white dove was observed floating above her body. One night later, when her body was taken by a monk and placed in the boat of a fisherman, the white dove appeared again. The fisherman followed the dove as the bird skimmed the waters, leading him to Monaco, and he buried the girl's body there.

I wondered if my stay in Monaco would be as incredible.

Eight

My suite had a sweeping view of the sparkling sea and the towering cliffs that soared for miles along the curving coastline. As I unpacked my bags, showered, and changed, I could hear Helga moving about in her suite next door. From the sounds of her movements, I could tell that her actions roughly duplicated mine.

It was several hours before play would resume at the casino. We would, of course, dine at the hotel's penthouse restaurant with the sliding ceiling that opened to the sky. But there was plenty of time to spend before dinner. I knew Helga didn't care about sightseeing, and I thought it would be a shame if we didn't enjoy this time together in a more pleasurable pursuit. Hoping that Helga felt the same way, I solved the minor but potentially troublesome difficulty presented by the locked door between us by ordering champagne, caviar, and three dozen red roses to be delivered to her at six. At approximately one minute after the hour, she rapped on the door and called to me softly.

"You are very thoughtful," she said, holding out a glass of champagne as I entered her suite.

She was wearing a delicate pink negligee that outlined her body in a lovely silhouette when she moved to the windows overlooking the sea. I paused for a moment to enjoy the sight of her body through the gossamer fabric of the garment and then joined her at the window.

The setting sun had disappeared somewhere below the horizon, but it had left a deep, rich, golden reflection behind in the clear sky. The waters of the Mediterranean, in turn, reflected the sky, intensifying the light so that the room seemed to be alive with dazzling gold.

"It's a very lovely view, isn't it?" Helga asked, turning toward me.

"Yes, very lovely," I replied, my eyes deliberately running down the length of her body and up again until I met her gaze. She ran her tongue around her lips and asked, "Do you like me, Tony?"

"Yes, very much."

"As much as you like my sisters?" she persisted. The question surprised me after the night we had spent together in New York, but instead of answering her directly, I held out my arms and said, "Would you like me to show you how much?"

She came toward me in a sensuous, flowing motion, her eyes half closed and her lips parted. I kissed her, and her whole body immediately responded, vibrating gently up and down against me. Her legs opened and encircled mine, and I could feel her quivering center seeking my own aroused, responding body. She moaned softly and swayed backwards, setting down her champagne glass. I placed my own glass on a nearby table. When I turned back, I saw her slipping off her negligee.

The golden light turned her nude body into a exquisitely molded, living bronze statue. I barely had time to remove my own clothing before she had pulled me down onto the chaise lounge with her.

"Quickly!" she whispered, pleading, as she thrust her hips up. We were joined.

"Yes! Yes! Yes!" she murmured breathlessly. Her hands clutched at my shoulders and arms, and her nails dug into my flesh as she urged me on. Moments later, I felt her body opening and closing around me, her head twisting from side to side in passion, until we reached the peak of a wildly convulsive climax.

As we lay side by side on the chaise, she turned her head and looked at me. She was smiling softly, "You know now, don't you?"

I nodded.

I knew what I should have guessed ever since we had left New York—but, of course, until a few minutes ago there had been no way to tell. The woman lying beside me was not Helga, for

I was familiar with her distinctive way of making love. Nor was it Maria, whom I also knew intimately.

"You're Elsa."

"Yes," she admitted. "You're not sorry, are you?"

"How can you ask a question like that? After what we just shared?"

She laughed delightedly. "Helga will be furious when she finds out what I've done. I was spending the night in her apartment when you phoned her in the morning. She was still asleep and didn't hear a thing. When you suggested a trip to Monte Carlo, I just decided to pack up and go and let you think I was Helga. It sounded like such fun. Besides, you've already spent enough time with my two sisters. It's my turn."

As I listened to her words, I reflected that it was just the kind of trick that the Von Alder women were capable of playing. But even though her explanation did sound plausible enough, I had to remind myself that the Von Alders were suspects in the case I was trying to solve and that there might be something sinister in Elsa's substitution for Helga.

But I could do nothing at that moment. I smacked lightly on her shapely little buttocks and told her to get dressed.

When we arrived at the casino after dinner, we found it was jammed. The huge crowd was standing in a tightly packed circle around one roulette wheel in hushed anticipation. There were three men inside the circle: the croupier, a second man, who wore a tuxedo and dark glasses—obviously one of the directors—and the Belgian, Tregor, the man who was breaking the bank.

Elsa and I managed to squeeze through the crowd to a spot only a few feet away from the three men. Just as we arrived, the spinning roulette wheel clicked to a stop, and the watching crowd pressed forward and gasped. The croupier shoved a mountainous stack of chips across the table to Tregor, who imperturbably put them beside another huge stack in front of him.

"My God!" a woman near me whispered excitedly. "He just won half a million dollars! What's he going to do now?"

Tregor seemed oblivious to the people pressed around him. He was a giant, imposing man with a big belly who sipped from a glass of mineral water he kept filled from a bottle standing at his elbow. Dark glasses hid his eyes, but his face, I noticed, was set in an absolutely blank mask.

Every eye in the room was trained on him, waiting to see what he'd do next. He leaned forward and rested his forehead on the fist he had made with his right hand as if he was meditating and remained in that posture for several seconds. At that moment I was probably the only one in the crowd who glanced toward the director standing opposite. He was in almost the identical pose as Tregor! It was almost as if they were silently communicating with one another!

A second later both men raised their heads simultaneously, and Tregor with a steady hand confidently placed his whole stack of chips on the red square in front of him.

Elsa clutched my arm. "He's going to bet all his winnings!" she whispered unbelievingly. "A million dollars!"

Tregor settled back into his chair as the croupier raised a hand and set the wheel spinning again. It spun dizzily for a second or two. As it began to slow, the onlookers started chanting in unison, "Red, red, red"—Tregor's bet. Finally the wheel stopped. The Belgian had won again. The croupier pushed another stack of chips toward Tregor's original stack. Two million dollars! Then the director stepped forward and announced in a quiet voice, "The wheel is closed for the evening."

The crowd moved back as Tregor collected his chips with the help of several casino employees and headed toward the cashier. I noticed that at least twelve secret agents from various foreign governments, all of whom I recognized, were trailing him. Tregor wouldn't, he couldn't, go anywhere without those agents right behind him. The world's governments had made it difficult for him to slip out of town easily.

I considered all modes of transportation in and out of Monte Carlo. There were only three roads that led out of the town, and they could be easily watched. The town officials kept all boats in the harbor under constant surveillance, and they had the fastest boat in the Mediterranean. No one could leave by air because there is no level stretch of ground in Monte Carlo long enough to make an airfield. These factors would prevent Tregor from eluding the agents who were trailing him to find out where he was taking the money he had won. It wasn't necessary for me to follow.

I was interested in the director and the croupier, who were now dismantling the roulette wheel—a common practice at the close of play when the house has suffered such enormous losses. The wheel would be carried to the casino basement where all the casino's wheels, which are made of rosewood, are manufactured. Each wheel, I knew, was balanced to an exactitude of one thousandth of an inch and moved on jewels as precisely as a watch.

But a wheel could be fixed. That's why I wanted a closer look at this particular one and why I followed the director and the croupier when they went through a nearby door. As I watched them disappear through the doorway, I instructed Elsa to go back to the hotel and to wait for me there.

It was dark on the stairs that led to the basement, but there was a light below. I'd gotten half-way down the stairs when the door above me slammed shut. At the same moment a blinding light snapped on. Then I heard a shrill scream. Turning quickly, I saw that Elsa, contrary to my instructions, had followed me. A man, probably the one who had slammed the door, had her in a tight grip and was pointing a gun at me.

I turned back toward the basement to see the casino director and the croupier climbing the stairs toward me. Both carried guns, and the croupier also carried a length of pipe in one hand. When the two men had reached the step below me, the director whipped off his dark glasses. His eyes were glazed as if he were hypnotized or drugged. "Take care of him," he ordered. The croupier raised the iron pipe, and everything went black.

Consciousness returned slowly, and even when I was able to see and hear again, it was as if I were viewing my surroundings from a distance and through a hazy filter. My body and limbs felt heavy and sluggish. Although rough hands were shoving me, I hardly felt a thing. Gradually I recognized the symptoms of my lethargic condition. I had been heavily drugged while I had been unconscious. It must have been one of the powerful depressants that work on the central nervous system.

I was fighting hard to overcome the effect of the drugs, but even though I was in excellent physical shape, I was only partially succeeding. I could see all that was going on around me but could not move. The croupier and the director had placed me behind the steering wheel in the front seat of a car. I saw Elsa, drugged and unconscious, sprawled in the seat beside me, and there were men leaning inside both opened doors. The motor of the Mercedes was racing, but the car wasn't moving.

Then I noticed that one of the men was adjusting something around the floorboards under my feet. Soon he slid out of the car, and I heard him say, "Okay, she's ready to take off."

The car doors were slammed shut. The engine was still racing. My drugged brain couldn't determine the meaning of what was happening. Dimly, as if I were in the midst of a fog, I saw a hand reach in through the open window next to me and put the Mercedes in gear. The car shot forward.

Then I realized that Elsa and I had been placed in the Mercedes with the accelerator pressed to the floorboards. We were now streaking along the dark, deserted roads of Monaco at over a hundred miles an hour. At that accelerated speed, the Mercedes would crash before we had gone too far, and we'd both be killed. When our bodies were found, it would look like we had died in an accident after an overdose of drugs. There would be no indication of murder.

Desperately I tried to gain control of my body.

So far, we had been lucky and the car had stayed at the center of the road. But up ahead there would be hills and curves, and unless I could begin steering the car, we'd go off the side of the road soon. I tried to raise my hands, but they felt like heavy weights. I tried again. Both hands rose ponderously, faltered, dropped, and rose again slowly. I could see the dark landscape sweeping past in a blinding blur from the car window.

Sweat was pouring from my body from the effort of lifting my hands a few inches to the steering wheel. Then I saw a sharp curve ahead. I could see my fingers closed around the steering wheel, but I couldn't feel the wheel under them. Somehow I managed to turn it a few degrees to the right just as the car went into the S-curve. It was enough to keep us on the road. The car whipped around the curve at break-neck speed and catapulted over the top of a steep incline.

The road continued to climb. From the car window I saw that we were on the precipice of a cliff that fell almost straight down from the edge of the pavement to the sea. The car crested on the top of the precipice and then careened along the steep angle toward the road like a metal projectile shot from a cannon. The tires shrieked against the pavement. Still dulled by the drugs, I tried to concentrate on our one chance of survival: somehow I had to keep the car upright and on the road until it finally ran out of gas.

There seemed no end to the nightmare that followed. Mile after mile the Mercedes roared past darkened villas and cottages, up and down the winding, twisting roads of the Cote d'Azur. Monaco was far behind us. We sped along the corniches, the highways linking Monaco to Nice and then through Nice itself, silent and shuttered for the night.

The highway beyond Nice ran level with the sea—wet and slick and dangerous. The rear of the Mercedes slipped from one side to the other. If we skidded, we would land in the sea. But the Mercedes streaked on through Antibes. Finally, somewhere between Antibes and Cannes, it began to lose speed, and in another mile or so it was barely rolling. With a tremendous effort I twisted the steering wheel, and the car lunged to the side of the road and stopped. The engine went dead. Elsa, still on the seat next to me, hadn't stirred once.

Nine

The sun was streaming into my eyes. I groaned and sat up, rubbing the back of my neck. The Mercedes was still by the side of the road. The first thing I saw was Elsa putting on her make-up. Then I saw a crowd of children outside the window on Elsa's side pressed close to the glass, staring at her with wide eyes as she powdered her nose. She looked great—as if she had just awakened from a refreshing sleep. Trucks and cars were whizzing past on the highway, and I saw that most of the passengers inside them were craning their necks to get a better look at us.

Elsa noticed that I was sitting up, put her compact and lipstick away, and smiled.

"Did we have fun last night?" she asked brightly.

I didn't know how much she knew or remembered of the previous evening when we had been roughed up on the basement stairs of the casino. The whole night had been a nightmare to me, but I had to give the Von Alder women credit for one thing—they were resilient.

"Come on," I said as I leaned past her to open the door on her side. She climbed out of the car, and I followed. "We've got to get back to Monte Carlo. This car is out of gas."

"But how are we going to get there?"

"Leave that to me," I said, pulling her up beside me on the edge of the highway. The children were still flocking around us. I positioned Elsa in front of me where she could be easily seen by the passing traffic and elevated my thumb in the international hitchhikers' sign. The first vehicle to come along braked to a stop, and the driver, rattling away in French, swung the door open.

"Monte Carlo," I said.

"Oui," he said. Elsa and I, riding up front beside the driver, returned to Monte Carlo in a produce truck filled with *aubergine*—eggplant. The doorman at the Hotel de Paris did not lift an eyebrow as we, still in our evening attire, alighted from the truck, waved and thanked the truck driver, and swept through the lobby.

I left Elsa at the door of her suite and told her to get some rest. As I entered my rooms, I heard the phone ringing. It was the local AXE agent, a man known to me as Chiclet. He said I was needed at the local AXE office immediately to receive a telephone call from overseas. Hawk was probably calling from the states on a scrambler phone. I changed clothes hurriedly—even in Monaco a dinner jacket in the daytime would call unwanted attention to me—and went to the AXE office, which was in a villa not far from the hotel.

Chiclet met me at the door and drew me to one side to talk. The place was swarming with the same agents I had seen at the casino, the men assigned to trail Tregor when he left with his winnings.

Before I asked Chiclet about Tregor, I gave him a quick account of what had happened to me and Elsa and asked if we could have the casino director and the croupier picked up immediately.

Chiclet shook his head. "I'm afraid that would be difficult," he said sadly. "Both have vanished—along with Tregor."

"Vanished?" I asked incredulously. "How could Tregor vanish with all those agents tailing him?"

"We are up against some very crafty intelligence," Chiclet explained. "Last night when Tregor left the casino, he went back to his hotel. We had men there watching the place at the front and rear. Other agents were in position at the roads leading out of town and along the harbor. But Tregor, the casino director, and the croupier eluded all of them."

"How did they do it?"

Chiclet shook his head, as if he still disbelieved it. "Tregor's room had a balcony facing toward the sea. Some time in the early hours of the morning a helicopter swooped in over the city.

It lifted Tregor from the balcony and apparently picked up the others somewhere else in town and flew away. An amazing occurrence."

I agreed.

"We may not turn up anything," Chiclet went on, "but we're checking up and down the coast to see if anyone heard the helicopter. If so, they might be able to give us a lead on the direction that it took."

"And if we don't turn up anyone who heard the copter, we're right back where we started," I added. Then I reminded Chiclet that he had told me I'd be getting a call from overseas.

He nodded. "Hawk wants to talk to you on a scrambled wire. I'll tell the operator to put the call through." He led me to an upstairs office, and when Hawk came on the line, he left me alone.

"I hear your quarry slipped away," Hawk said without preamble. "Any further developments?"

"None," I told him before I gave him a full report on my own experiences of the previous night.

Hawk snorted. "Sounds like you had a close call." He paused, and the wires between us hummed briefly. Then he said, "Something happened here that I wanted you to know about. Your hunch about autopsying Z1's brain paid off. Dr. Tom did find something—a small microscopic disc embedded in the base of the brain. We don't know what it is or what it means. The lab boys are trying to analyze it now. And Dr. Tom can't figure out how it got there. There are no marks or signs of an operation on the skull."

"Still it must mean something," I said.

"Possibly," Hawk answered vaguely. "When we find more, if we do, I'll let you know. What are your plans now?"

"I want to try to pick up the trail of that helicopter and the money," I told him. "Both are probably still somewhere in the area. The money could lead me to whoever's at the source of all this. Anyway, it's the only promising lead I've had so far."

"Yes, well, good hunting," Hawk said and hung up.

Chiclet was waiting for me in a room downstairs that was filled with men talking on telephones in rapid French and Italian. One wall was covered with a large map showing Monaco and the area surrounding it from the Gulf of Lyon on the French coast on the west to the Gulf of Genoa on the Italian coast on the east. Colored pins were stuck in the map at various points outside of Monaco.

"My agents are making some progress," Chiclet said, nodding toward the men on the phones. "You see," he pointed to the map on the wall, "we've been contacting authorities in towns along the coast in both directions to question local citizens if they heard a helicopter during the night. Now we're beginning to get some calls back with the results."

"Any positive answers?"

"Fortunately, yes," Chiclet answered, guiding me over to the wall map. He pointed to the pins. "So far, we have had reports from St. Raphael and Fréjus that a helicopter was heard. Reports from the east, from Italy, are negative. Apparently, our men headed westward. Now we're concentrating on the coast beyond Fréjus." He smiled. "Soon we may be able to pinpoint exactly where they went."

I looked at the map. West of Fréjus, along the curving coastline, were St. Tropez, Hyeres, La Seyne, and, farther on, Marseille. But something else caught my eye on the map—a group of islands, Iles d'Hyeres, off the coast halfway between Fréjus and Marseille. I began to think.

"Look, Chiclet," I said, "it's important that I get a helicopter and pilot immediately. Can you arrange it?"

"Certainly. It will take a while, but let me put in a call."

He used one of the phones and came back, nodding. "There will be a helicopter here within the hour. One of our agents from Nice will be flying it." He looked at me quizzically. "You have a plan?"

"The way I figure it," I said, "is that that helicopter didn't go far—it had never planned to, never really could. My guess is that it landed somewhere near here where it could be hidden and that the money and the men will probably be transferred from it tonight."

"Transferred?" Chiclet asked, puzzled. "To what?"

I shrugged. "Your guess is as good as mine. But I would think they would use a fast boat."

"A fast boat!" Chiclet exclaimed. "Of course. That would be the obvious thing to do."

Pointing to the map, I added, "And that makes me think that perhaps the whirlybird we're looking for might be hidden somewhere around those islands, the Iles d'Hyeres, or along the coast. Wherever it is, it'll be easier to spot from another helicopter that is flying low than from the ground."

Chiclet agreed with my reasoning. While we waited for the helicopter to arrive, I phoned Elsa at the Hotel de Paris and told her I was going to be tied up for a while on some business but that I wanted her to wait for me there.

"I was going to surprise you," she said, pouting. "I slipped into your room, but you weren't there. Are you sure you're occupied with business?"

"Of course," I assured her. "You just stay put until I get there. It may be later today, or tonight. Then we'll have plenty of time for surprises."

Ten

Since it was inadvisable to attract too much attention in Monaco, Chiclet drove me out of town to a place in the hills where we waited for the helicopter. Before we left the office, more reports had come in that indicated that no helicopter had been heard during the night west of Fréjus. It looked like I might have guessed right—that the helicopter had taken cover somewhere nearby.

"You will be careful now," Chiclet advised anxiously. "You don't know what kind of odds you'll be up against."

I nodded. I had my faithful Luger, Wilhelmina, fitted snugly in my shoulder holster, and my stiletto, Hugo, was in its own sheath under my coat sleeve, ready to spring into my hand with the slightest move of my arm. I didn't worry much about the odds.

It wasn't long before the helicopter that we had been waiting for arrived. It was a UH-1 Huey chopper. Chiclet introduced me to the pilot, a young Frenchman named Marcel Clement, a big, rangy, tousled-haired man who smiled easily.

Chiclet instructed him that he was to follow my orders and warned him that the job could be dangerous.

"Danger doesn't bother me, Chiclet," the pilot assured him. "You know that."

I climbed into the chopper, but before we took off, Chiclet made a circular tour around the craft to be satisfied that it was in top working order. Then he waved us away. Marcel sat in the forward bubble-nose of the helicopter, and I sat behind with the doors slid back so that I had a clear view below with the pair of powerful binoculars that Chiclet had given me.

We headed west, following the shore line. After we had passed Fréjus, Marcel flew low while both he and I scoured the ground for some sign of a place where the helicopter might be hidden. We passed a few spots where the foliage was dense and other places where there were recesses in the cliffs—places where the copter could be concealed—but I could spot nothing to indicate that any of them was the hiding place. By then we had traveled the whole length of the coast from Monaco to a point far beyond Fréjus where there had been reports of a helicopter during the night. The cluster of islands, Îles d'Hyeres, was visible to the south.

"Let's go out and make a swing over there," I shouted to Marcel, pointing seaward.

He nodded and veered the helicopter. Soon we

were over the islands and making another low-level sweep over the terrain. The binoculars gave me a close-up view of everything below, including some of the residents of the island who waved cheerily to us, but we saw no sign of the elusive helicopter.

"What now?" Marcel asked from the cockpit.

"Might as well take us back," I said reluctantly.

Marcel put the copter into a turn to head back to shore. I was still studying the area with the binoculars when suddenly I spotted a small dark speck in the sea. When I focused on it, I saw another small island, rocky and barren, except for a few trees and some sparse undergrowth. It was so small that it hadn't been recorded on the map in Chiclet's office. Nevertheless, it was still large enough—a mile to a mile and a half square—for a helicopter to land, and it was also remote enough from the mainland to make a good hiding place.

I tapped Marcel on the shoulder and pointed to the island. "What's that place there? Are you familiar with it?"

"It is called 'Satané Roc,' " Marcel said, " 'Devil Rock,' a name given to it by the French underworld, who used it years ago as a transfer point for guns and drugs flowing into the country. The authorities put an end to their operations a long time ago. Since then, it's been deserted, except, I've heard, for a colony of rats that infests the place. They say the rats got there from some shipwreck long ago and have multiplied in the years since."

"I think we should take a closer look at it," I said.

"You think our men might be hiding there?" Marcel asked doubtfully.

"It's possible. It's just possible."

Marcel turned the copter seaward again. We passed over Iles d'Hyeres once more and continued southward. As we got closer to *Satané Roc*, I could see what a bleak, forbidding place it was, with nothing more than a pile of black rocks jutting up out of the sea and, here and there, a few scrawny trees and patches of waist-high brush. *Satané Roc*—a suitable name.

Marcel took the helicopter down until we brushed the treetops to make a slow, circular sweep of the island. As we flew close to the ground, I could see hundreds of large black rats, frightened by the sound of our engine, scurrying among the rocks.

"You see anything?" Marcel asked.

"Rats," I answered. "Swarms of rats."

We had almost completed our circle when I suddenly spotted something with the binoculars. It was a brilliant flash of light, the reflection of sun on metal, beneath one of the large outcroppings of rocks in the center of the island. It could be the hidden helicopter.

I told Marcel what I had seen and asked him to circle the place once more.

He nodded and banked the copter, and we started back toward the spot. Marcel was flying so low that we nearly brushed the tops of the trees below. I had my binoculars trained on the spot where I thought I had seen something and was concentrating so hard that I had no thought of danger until Marcel screamed. Suddenly I felt the helicopter lurch and sputter.

In the next second we were assailed by a barrage of bullets that slammed into the helicopter from below, smashing the glass shield of the cockpit, ripping through the copter's metal exterior, and thudding into the motor. As I crouched behind the cockpit, I could see four or five men firing at us with upraised submachine guns from the top of some rocks.

"Marcel!" I yelled, grabbing him by the shoulder, "Get us out of here."

When he turned toward me in his seat, I saw that his face was a bloody mask. He tried to say something, but only blood came from his mouth. His eyes closed, and he toppled sideways from his seat. I grabbed Wilhelmina from its holster, but before I had time to aim and fire at the men below, the helicopter engine blew up in a great flaming fireball. The machine plunged toward the sea, trailed by a giant sheet of flame and smoke.

The low altitude saved my life. I jammed the

Luger back into the holster and jumped through the open doorway to avoid the flames just before the helicopter hit the water. The fire and smoke surrounding the copter screened me from the sight of the men who had shot us down. When I surfaced, I found that I was still hidden from the view of those on the island, the flaming helicopter, still floating on the surface of the sea, was between me and land.

I rapidly calculated the distance to the island, dove deep, and swam underwater until I felt that my lungs would burst. I kept swimming until I finally scraped up against some rocks. Feeling my way inch by inch up the rocks with my hands, I eventually broke through the surface of the water soundlessly. With only my head above water, I pressed myself flat against the rocks and gulped down air. When I was able to breathe normally again, I cautiously raised my head and looked around.

Fortunately, as I had hoped, I had come to shore a good distance from where the helicopter had crashed. From that point, I could still see the charred remains of the copter floating on the water. I watched as several of the men who had been on the island set out in rubber rafts and paddled toward the wreckage. I saw them remove Marcel's body and place it in one of the rafts. Afterwards the men searched the water around the wreckage. They had obviously seen two men in the helicopter and were hoping to find my corpse, too. I was careful to keep low in the water and to remain partially hidden by the rocks until they had given up their search.

As the men paddled back to the island, the smoldering heap of metal that had once been the helicopter sank beneath the surface of the water. I clung to the rocks until the men had pulled their rubber rafts on shore and had returned to the center of the island. I briefly considered swimming down the shore to one of the rafts so that I could try to make it back to the mainland. But then I remembered the urgency of my assignment. The men on the island, and the money they had taken from the casino, might lead me to something vital.

I would wait until the light had begun to fade, and then I would try to make my way across the island to assess the situation.

From what I'd observed, it appeared that the men were using the island temporarily while they waited to be picked up after dark by a boat.

Eleven

After another hour, the late afternoon sun began to set, and I felt it was safe to crawl up the rocks to dry off in the warm breeze that was blowing in from the south. I had just climbed up on the rocks and stretched out on a narrow ledge when I felt something soft drop on my left leg. I jumped up to find myself staring into the blood-red, beady eyes of a large black rat that had apparently fallen from a higher rock. I kicked out at it and shook it loose and sent it scurrying away by tossing a rock.

Then I heard soft squealing sounds all around me. I stood up quickly and saw dozens of shiny, unblinking eyes. A cold shiver ran down my spine, and my hand went instinctively for the Luger, Wilhelmina. For a moment, I didn't care if a shot would bring the men on the island looking for me.

But the rats didn't attack. Instead, they scurried nervously back and forth, squealing softly, their claws scratching the surface of the rocks. I backed away warily, keeping my eyes on the horde, until I felt a hard, round metal object poking into my back between my shoulder blades. A harsh voice snarled, "Just stand right there!"

A hand reached from behind me and took the Luger. Then the man—it was the croupier from the casino—stepped in front of me. He was holding a snubnosed .38 in one hand and my Luger in the other. He nodded at me. "We thought you had gotten out of the helicopter alive. We've been looking for you. Start walking."

He leaned down and picked up a hunk of wood that had evidently been doused with gasoline. After lighting one end of it so that it became a flaming torch, he waved it around to clear a path through the swarm of rats, who scurried frantically away into the brush.

We climbed higher up the rocks of the island until we reached the large outcropping that I had spotted from the air. The croupier waved his gun and shoved me forward into a large hollowed-out cavern. Flaming torches were set in a circle around the entrance to keep the rats out, and their light revealed the helicopter inside. The other men were there, too—the casino director, Tregor, and the man who had grabbed Elsa on the basement stairs of the casino. I guessed that he must have been the one who had piloted the helicopter.

The others regarded me without much interest, but the casino director nodded to the croupier,

"Search him, tie him up, and keep your eye on him."

The croupier, still holding the gun on me, reached inside the helicopter and drew out a couple of lengths of rope. Then he prodded me deeper into the interior of the cavern. I raised my hands when he started to search me so that he missed finding the stilleto, Hugo, set on a spring in the arm sheath inside my coat sleeve. After the search, he made me stretch out on the ground while he tied me up securely with the rope.

I would have to bide my time. For the moment, with the croupier standing nearby holding the gun and watching me, I was helpless. But I still had Hugo up my sleeve.

It was getting dark outside. From time to time, one of the men would take a pair of binoculars and a flashlight and go outside. It didn't take me long to realize that they were waiting to be taken from the island. My original theory seemed correct—a boat was going to pick them up.

An hour or more passed before one of the men on lookout shouted, and the others, except for the croupier who was still guarding me, hurried out. I used that moment, when my captor's attention was temporarily diverted, to snap the spring in the knife sheath. The stilleto slipped instantly into my right hand. I had to cut through the ropes quickly. I had just managed to sever them and free my hands when the three men hurried back into the cave.

"He's here," the director shouted. "We'll ditch the helicopter and come back for you."

"How do I know you will return?" the croupier asked suspiciously.

The director had taken a large aluminum suitcase from the helicopter. He placed it on the floor of the cave and nodded toward it. "The money will still be here. We'll be back."

All of the men began to push the helicopter from the cavern. While their attention was diverted, I rolled onto my side and arched my body backwards so that my hands could reach the ropes that were binding my legs. Soon I was free, and I returned to my former position, lying still while I tried to work my arms and legs behind my back to restore the circulation. By then the men had shoved the helicopter out of the cave and the croupier had returned to my side. The voices of the other three were becoming faint in the distance.

My guardian glanced at me briefly. Then he dug a cigarette out of his pocket and lit a match. I made my move, springing to my feet and lunging across to him, holding the stilletto in my hand. I flashed the knife in the startled man's face and then poked the point gently into his belly, and with my free hand I reached for the gun.

Instead of obeying me, he foolishly raised his

gun to fire. I plunged the stilletto into his mid-section, and he doubled over without a sound, the lighted cigarette still dangling from his lips. I hadn't planned to kill him, but he had given me no choice.

I grabbed his .38 and my Luger and rushed quickly to the aluminum suitcase. I snapped open the lock, and the top sprang up. There in the wavering light of the torches I looked down at the two million dollars inside.

I had devised a little plan for that money ever since the director had set the suitcase down and I had known that it was there. I hastily began to execute it. I scooped out the stacks of bills and filled the bottom of the suitcase with large rocks from the floor of the cave. Then I spread a layer of bills, no more than a couple of hundred dollars, over the rocks. I snapped the suitcase shut and left it in its original place.

I could still hear the voices of the other men faintly in the distance as I quickly unbuttoned my shirt, stuffed the money inside, buttoned up again. Two million dollars against my chest was clumsy, but, weighted down as I was, I returned to the dead croupier, grabbed him by the back of the collar, and dragged him across the cave to the outside.

The other three men were still working with the helicopter on the other side of the large flat rock outcropping. I struck out in the opposite direction, dragging the corpse behind me, until I reached some deep brush where I could hide it. Then I crawled back across the rock to a high spot where I could observe the action below.

The full moon clearly illuminated the scene. By now they had pushed the chopper into a clearing. One of the men, the pilot, climbed into it and set the rotor blades in motion. The copter began to rise, but when it was a few feet off the ground, the man jumped out. The pilotless helicopter suddenly shot into the air, streaked away from the rock, and plunged into the dark waters below. It sank without a trace.

Meanwhile the casino director had returned to the cave. He came running out, carrying the suitcase and shouting. I could hear the voices of the men distinctly where I was hiding, and I heard the director yell, "He's escaped! That fellow cut himself free and got away! He took Georges with him!"

"The money? The money?" Tregor yelled back. "Is the money safe?"

The director set the suitcase on the ground, and all three of them crowded around him when he opened it.

"It's here! It's still here!" he exclaimed. As I had hoped, he didn't take the time to examine the money beyond the top layer of bills, since the load of rocks approximated the weight of the real bills.

"Come on!" Tregor yelled. "Let's get off this damned island."

The three began to signal with their flashlights. An answering signal came from just off the edge of the island, and a giant searchlight was snapped on. Then I saw that instead of a boat, it was a seaplane that would be taking them away. It had taxied in near the rocks and was waiting there, bobbing up and down on the water. As the men began to make their way down to the plane, I heard them speculate about me.

"Where do you think that fellow and Georges disappeared to?"

"He probably forced Georges to take him down to one of the rafts so he could get back to the mainland."

I stayed where I was, watching until they reached the edge of the island, got into one of the rafts there, and paddled out to the plane. I didn't feel safe until they were aboard, and the plane had taken off and disappeared to the north.

I hoped they wouldn't discover that almost all the money was missing until they had reached their destination. By that point, it would be dangerous for them to return since they couldn't be sure I hadn't reached the mainland to bring back the authorities. I was still no closer to solving the case, but at least, I had managed to thwart their plans.

Twelve

The moon set soon after the plane left. It was now so dark that I could scarcely see my hand in front of my face. I tried to find the croupier's body where I had left it in the brush, but that proved to be an impossible task in the darkness. As much as I disliked the idea of spending the night on that island infested with rats, I knew it would be too risky in the darkness to try to make my way to the edge of the shore to look for one of the rubber rafts. I decided to return to the cave where a couple of the torches that the men had set up were still burning.

As I returned to the cave, I gathered up an armful of dry brush along the way and carried it back with me. I fed the dry brush into the flaming torches until there was a low flame as I sat huddled up at the entrance. It was the only way I could keep the swarming rats at bay, but I could still see their eyes gleaming in the firelight beyond the cave. I kept my Luger in my hand, and although I was tired, I didn't dare doze off for fear that the rats would grow bold and attack.

It seemed like an endless time before dawn finally came. I was up on my feet and preparing to make my way down to the water with the first light. I checked to make sure the money was still safely buttoned up inside my shirt, and then, carrying a burning torch to keep the rats away, I set out. Before I started down the side of the island, however, I checked in the brush to find the croupier's body. I didn't find the corpse. There was only his skeleton with the bones picked clean. The rats had been at work in the dark.

I turned hastily away and hurried down through the brush while the rats scurried out of my way before me. I had just reached the edge of the island and had started to search for one of the rafts when I heard a humming sound from the water. When I looked, I saw a large white cruiser circling about a quarter of a mile away. At first I thought the men from the night before had returned to try to find me and the money, but when I took a closer cool, I saw that the cruiser was the police boat from Monaco. I quickly fired several shots into the air from the Luger.

The cruiser heard my signal and immediately veered toward the shore. When it dropped anchor, three men lowered a dinghy and rowed in to get me. I was surprised to see that one of the men was Chiclet. How had he known where to look for me?

"Well," Chiclet greeted me, "you've turned up alive after all. We had almost given you up for lost. Tell me, what happened?"

I gave him a quick summary of the events and showed him the money I recovered. Before we left the island, we went back up the rocks and brought the croupier's skeleton down to the dinghy. Then we cast off, leaving *Satané Roc* to the rodent colony.

When we were aboard the cruiser, headed back to Monaco, Chiclet told me how he had found me. "Before you and Marcel took off in the helicopter yesterday," he said, "I placed a beeper on the copter's tail. I've been receiving a signal ever since you took off. When you didn't return by nightfall, I alerted the police and asked to have the boat standing by at dawn. We followed the signal from the beeper, and it led us to this point just off the island where we found the helicopter underwater. The beeper still works. But I must say I was afraid you were dead when I realized the helicopter had gone into the sea."

"I'm sorry about Marcel," I told Chiclet. "He was a good pilot and a brave man."

Chiclet nodded. "I'm sorry, too. But he knew the risks just as we all do."

When we reached Monte Carlo, Chiclet made

5

arrangements to return the money to the casino while I made another overseas call to Hawk on a scrambled wire from his office. I told Hawk what had happened and how I had recovered the money.

"Well," Hawk said more heartily than I think he felt, "at least everything didn't go against us. If the pattern continues as it has in the past, it probably won't be long before there's a new development. And Nick—"

"Yes sir?" I asked.

"I want you to take it easy for a day or two, get some rest." He paused and added gruffly, "That's an order. I'll be in touch with you."

Before I could answer, he hung up.

The police had already transferred the croupier's remains to the local morgue and the money was on its way back to the casino. There was nothing more for me to do at the AXE office. I told Chiclet that I was going back to the hotel to sleep.

Elsa was waiting for me in my suite when I arrived. At first she pretended to be angry with me, but when she noticed how exhausted I looked, her mock petulance turned to sympathetic concern.

"Poor Dumplink," she cooed, "you look a terrible sight. What have you been doing?"

"It was an all-night business session," I told

her, as I removed my jacket and tie. "And now I need a good hot shower and a long sleep."

"Of course, Dumplink," she said. "You get undressed. I'll start the shower for you."

Before I could protest, she had disappeared into the bath and turned on the shower.

By the time I had changed into my robe the bathroom was full of steam. Elsa emerged, pink-cheeked, pushed me in the shower, and closed the door.

I scrubbed every inch of my skin and hair under the stinging hot water and then rinsed off with an ice cold shower. Afterwards I tied a fresh towel around my waist and went back to the bedroom. Elsa had pulled the spread down on the bed and was standing beside it.

"Sretch out, face-down," she ordered, patting the bed. When I hesitated, she gave me a light push. As I sprawled on the bed on my stomach, she whisked the towel away, saying, "Relax now, I give you a massage."

She produced a small bottle of lotion that she had brought from her suite, with a pungent lemon odor. Then she slipped off her robe, straddled my body, and began to apply the lotion to my back and shoulder blades. It was an astringent solution that first made my skin tingle and then sent a deep, soothing warmth into my muscles.

"What's that stuff you're using?" I asked, turning my head to look at Elsa as she leaned forward over me.

"It's an old Von Alden home remedy," she answered. "Guaranteed to give beneficial results."

Her caressing hands kneaded my flesh like a healing balm, moving up and down as lightly as a warm, sweet breath over the length of my body. Then Elsa raised to her knees and ordered me to roll over.

I faced her and lay between her spread legs. She began to lubricate the front of my body, her lightly tracing fingers circling, moving from my chest to my stomach, to my groin, down the sides of my legs to my toes. When she leaned close over me, her soft hair brushed against my bare flesh, and my nostrils were filled with its perfumed scent. For a long time, she seemed to work with an intense concentration that was almost hypnotic, but soon I became aware that her breathing was more rapid and her flesh had become moist and was quivering.

I raised my head and looked at her. Her eyes were wide and her lips were parted so that the tip of her pink tongue showed. I pulled her mouth to mine as I rolled her beneath me. Her arching hips strained upward. We met and joined silently and reached a climax simultaneously without a word.

I was more asleep than awake when our bodies parted. She stood up beside the bed, holding her robe. But when she leaned over and kissed me, I felt my body remembering again and was ready and eager for more. She laughed softly at the sight of my arousal and whispered, "I forgot to tell you, Dumplink, that sometimes that Von Alder remedy also acts as an aphrodisiac." She kissed me. "Sleep," she whispered.

I slept for twenty-four hours and might have slept longer if the ringing phone hadn't awakened me. It was Hawk calling.

"I hope you got some rest," he said. "I'm in Paris. Meet me here at the office as soon as you can. More bad news, I'm afraid. You might as well let the Von Alder woman come with you so you can keep an eye on her. I'll make reservations for both of you at the Hotel V George."

Elsa was pleased when I told her that I'd like her to accompany me to Paris. I phoned Chiclet to thank him and bid him farewell, and in less than an hour, Elsa and I were driving back to Nice to board the jet.

Thirteen

It was raining when we landed at Orly. As soon as I had deposited Elsa at the George V, where Hawk had reserved adjoining suites for us, I took a taxi to the Paris AXE office, which was located above a cafe on the Place St.-Michel. The offices were on the three top floors of the building and were soundproofed from the noise below. The proprietor of the establishment was an AXE agent whose code name was Bonaparte.

He greeted me at the door and led me to the stairs in the back that led to the offices above. As we passed through the smoky diningroom and bar, I was surprised to see that although there were many customers in the place, there were also some thirty or forty security police and AXE agents whom I recognized from previous encounters. I knew that something important must be taking place.

Hawk met me on the second floor. His face was grim, and he barely nodded as he led me into a private office and shut and locked the door.

"It looks like there's no end to this business,"

he said as he took an envelope from his pocket and passed it over to me. He stood with his back to me, looking out the window at the dark rain beating against the panes, while I read the letter inside the envelope.

The letter was typewritten: THE CHINESE NUCLEAR MISSILE WHICH DISAPPEARED 12 HOURS AGO WILL BE RETURNED IN EXCHANGE FOR $2,000,000. IF AGREEABLE, INSERT A CLASSIFIED AD IN THE LONDON TIMES TWO DAYS HENCE, READ: "ALEXANDER—TERMS ACCEPTED—(SIGNED) KUBLAI KHAN." FURTHER INSTRUCTIONS WILL FOLLOW.

The envelope had no address on it. Hawk, who had turned from the window, saw me frowning at the envelope and explained, "It was shoved under the door of the Chinese Embassy yesterday morning."

"And it's true that a Chinese nuclear missile disappeared?" I asked.

"All too true," Hawk answered bitterly. "It happened within hours after you turned over the money from Satané Roc. You will note that the sum requested is exactly the same as the amount recovered from the casino."

"You mean that a Chinese nuclear missile actually disappeared?" I was incredulous.

"Apparently," Hawk pointed out, "there is no limit to our enemy's ingenuity. Soon after your

experience on the island, the Chinese were flying
a nuclear missile to a secret testing site when the
plane simply vanished. Until this note arrived,
the Chinese thought the plane had crashed."

"What about the crew?" I asked, puzzled.
"They must have been well screened before they
were picked for an assignment like that."

"Oh, yes," Hawk agreed. "But it may be a
significant lead that only a few weeks ago, the
pilot, who was one of the most trusted and loyal
men in the Chinese airforce, was out of China on
an assignment to Albania. He wasn't watched
closely while he was there, and, in fact, the
Chinese cannot account for his activities during
several days of the visit. They are still checking.
It's probable that during that time he was reached
by our adversary who might have tampered with
his brain."

"Are the Chinese going to pay the ransom?" I
asked, handing the letter back to Hawk.

He nodded. "That's why we're meeting here
now. Come on upstairs."

On the top floor of the building, four Chinese
gentlemen, looking dour and a bit suspicious, were
waiting. Their presence explained the tight security in the building. One of the men was an interpreter and, through him, Hawk introduced me
to the other three whose names I recognized as
being high-ranking members of the Chinese Communist party. Each gave me a penetrating look

as we exchanged handshakes. Then all three spoke in rapid Chinese to the interpreter.

"They say," the interpreter said to me, "that they are honored to have such a distinguished representative aid them in recovering the nuclear missile. They also say that the chairman of the party has spoken with your president and that he has instructed them to cooperate with you in every way."

"I, too, am honored," I said to the interpreter. "I shall try to be worthy of the trust of the People's Republic."

That formality done, I asked, "Has a decision been made about paying the two million dollars?"

The interpreter conferred with his countrymen again and then handed me a large leather satchel that was engraved with Chinese characters and equipped with a lock. The interpreter unlocked it and opened to reveal packets of bills inside.

"Two million dollars," he said. "Tomorrow's edition of the London *Times* will carry the classified ad worded as the note instructed."

"All right," I said. "Lock the money up again. I want it to remain in your possession until we receive further word."

After the interpreter had translated my words, the three men bowed their heads gravely, and we again shook hands. Hawk told me that arrangements had already been made to have the Chinese representatives remain in the living quarters at the AXE office until there had been a response to the London *Times* ad. In that way, the ransom money would be well guarded until payoff time came.

Hawk rode back with me in a taxi to the hotel. It was dusk. The rain and the depressing weather seemed a perfect match for our moods.

"Whoever's behind this," Hawk muttered, "must be enjoying our predicament. Imagine stealing a nuclear missile and offering it back for ransom!"

"He chose some clever names for the ad," I remarked. "Alexander and Kublai Khan."

"He's a madman, but a very cunning one," Hawk observed. "What I wouldn't give to get my hands on him." He glanced at me.

When we reached the hotel, Hawk dropped me off and continued on to the American Embassy where he would be staying while in Paris.

When I reached my suite, I was surprised to find a note from Elsa. It said that she had been invited to a party in Montmartre and that she was going ahead. She left the address for me so that I could join her if I liked. I decided, instead, to have a couple of chilled martinis and a good dinner in my room. Before I went to bed, I phoned the desk to have a copy of the London *Times* delivered to me early the next morning.

Elsa still hadn't returned to the hotel by the time I received my copy of the newspaper early the next day, and I couldn't tell if there was any-

thing significant in her overnight absence. The
ad was there in the *Times*, though, worded exactly as the ransom note had instructed. As I
read it, I imagined a pleased "Alexander" reading
it too. He could be in Paris, or in London, or in
Monte Carlo, or, for that matter, in Tibet.

I was anxious to get to the AXE office, which,
I knew, would be the first place to know if further
instructions were received. I was dressed and
leaving the suite when Elsa returned.

She was still in an evening gown, with a mink
coat slung over her shoulders. She looked drowsy,
but she smiled and kissed me, letting the coat fall
to the floor. Then she turned for me to unzip the
back of her gown.

"I missed you at the party, Dumplink," she said.
"It was great fun. Lots of Frenchmen. The party's
still going on, if you want to go."

"No thanks," I said. "I have some business to
attend to. You sleep, and I'll phone you later."

"Business, business, business," she said, patting
my face. "Remember, all work and no play makes
Tony a dull boy." She stepped out of her gown
and crossed over to the connecting door to her
suite, looking very desirable in her sheer bra and
pantyhose. She paused briefly in the doorway and
beckoned to me with her finger. When I shook my
head, she blew me a kiss and disappeared.

Fourteen

As soon as I reached the cafe on Place St.-Michel and went upstairs to the AXE office, I could feel the tension and gloom that permeated the whole place. Outside the sun was shining and there was a false spring in the air, but whatever cheer the weather contained vanished at the walls of the building.

Hawk was there, looking more haggard than he had looked the night before, and so were the four Chinese, along with several dozen AXE agents and security men. All of us had arrived too early, and our impatience grew as the long hours dragged by. It wasn't until noon that we finally received the message we had been waiting for. And, of course, it came in a roundabout way.

We received a phone call from Interpol's Paris office, saying that they had received a package from a messenger for their local chief. When he had opened the package, he had found a sealed box and a typewritten note, which said that the box should be delivered to the Chinese Embassy at once. Since the chief of Interpol had been informed of the crisis, he had immediately called Hawk and had then sped to the AXE office. Meanwhile Interpol agents had picked up the messenger, who was authentic, and when they had questioned him about the man who had given him the package for delivery, he had given a description that could have fit ten thousand Frenchmen.

The box contained a recording tape. We crowded around while Hawk threaded the tape into an office machine. As the tape rolled, a voice said, "This is Alexander. I have received your message and now give you the following instructions. Late this afternoon, the thirtieth, a ship flying a white flag with a red dragon imprinted on it will appear in the Adriatic Sea and enter the harbor at Split, Yugoslavia. This ship will have the Chinese nuclear missile on its deck. One of your vessels may approach it with the two million dollars. Once the money has been placed in the hands of the men aboard, the missile will be returned. If any attempt is made to recover the missile without paying the money, it will be exploded."

The words on the tape told us nothing of the person who had spoken them—or, rather, persons, for every other sentence had been spoken by a different voice, and their accents had ranged from British to German to Brooklyn. The brains behind the plot had remained invisible.

After the tape had been transcribed and copies had been made, hurried phone calls were placed to secure a plane to fly us to the Adriatic coast and to have a large, fast ship waiting for us near Split, Yugoslavia. Even while these arrangements were being made, Hawk was busy making plans for the time when the missile had been recovered.

Not much later, Hawk, the Chinese representatives with ransom money, several AXE agents, and I drove to Orly and flew by jet to the Adriatic. The Yugoslavian Government had been contacted through diplomatic channels and had a sleek, swift ship waiting for us when we arrived.

There was a cold, bitter wind blowing off the sea as we approached the harbor and dropped anchor near the shore at Split. No other vessels were in sight. As we paced the deck, Hawk began to mutter, "I hope this isn't a trick, Nick."

After another couple of hours had passed and the day had started to fade into twilight, I was beginning to think that Hawk might have been right. But then, quite suddenly, a large white ship appeared at the mouth to the harbor, and it was flying a white flag with a red dragon emblazoned on it. It dropped anchor off the starboard bow of our vessel, and a man in a captain's uniform stepped to the rail, raised a bullhorn, and shouted, "Ahoy, I bring you greetings from Alexander. Do you have the money?"

Hawk handed me a similar bullhorn. "It's your show," he said.

"We have the money," I replied through the

bullhorn. "We are ready to complete the transaction."

"You may come aboard," the captain shouted back.

A couple of the crewmen aboard our ship lowered a small motorboat over the side. Two of the Chinese, one of them carrying the satchel with the money, and I crossed to the other ship. We were assisted to the deck by the captain and several of his crew. There was a huge object covered by lashed-down canvas on the forward deck. It must have been the missile, but I was still wary. Several other men were on deck, but the only one I recognized was Tregor, the Belgian.

The captain was cordial, and he led us to a large stateroom on the main deck where chilled champagne was waiting.

"You have the money?" he asked.

I nodded to the Chinese, who handed over the satchel.

"You have no objection to letting us count it before we turn the missile over to you, do you?" he asked.

"No," I replied.

"Please, gentlemen, do have some champagne while you're waiting," the captain offered as he left the room with the money.

Neither of the Chinese would accept a glass of champagne from the steward, but I did. It was good vintage wine and perfectly chilled. I had two glasses while the Chinese fidgeted uncomfortably in their chairs. When the captain returned he was smiling and nodding his head.

"Very good, gentlemen," he said. "All seems to be in order. If you'll accompany me to the deck, we can conclude our business."

I wasn't greatly surprised when we were topside again to see that the crewmen had removed the canvas from the object on the forward deck. It was a nuclear missile already fitted into a hoist.

The two Chinese checked the missile suspiciously before they were satisfied that all was in good order. They nodded to me gravely, and I nodded to the captain.

He seemed pleased as he picked up the bullhorn again and called to the waiting Yugoslavian ship, telling it to come in close so that the missile could be lowered to its decks. The two Chinese and I remained aboard while the crew worked the hoist, swinging the giant missile up into the air and then down to the deck of our ship where we had already prepared a cradle to hold it. I could see the expression of relief on Hawk's face when he saw the missile standing on the deck, safely aboard at last.

After the captain of the white ship and I had exchanged brief handshakes, I returned to our vessel with the Chinese.

"No trouble?" Hawk asked me at once.

"None," I said.

"If I know you, though," Hawk said, looking at me closely, "something's bothering you."

"It was all too simple." I replied. "They must know that since we've got the missile back safely, we aren't just going to sit here and let them sail away with the two million dollars."

"Perhaps they haven't thought of the plan we would use," Hawk said.

"I doubt that."

"Well, at any rate, they're pulling up anchor to leave," Hawk observed, pointing to the ship that was turning in the harbor. "I'm putting our plan into effect." He was holding a radio transmitter in his hand, and he began to speak into it rapidly, alerting all the vessels waiting just outside the harbor—Italian vessels, Greek ships, Yugoslavian, even some Russian cruisers—all those that had been sent in to apprehend our enemy.

As the white ship steamed toward the harbor mouth, we began to trail it at some distance. Just before it reached open sea, our armada of ships appeared. They were still distant, and Hawk hadn't yet ordered them to close in. The white ship suddenly came to a stop in the center of the mouth of the harbor. Hawk started to speak into the transmitter again, but I stopped him.

"Hold it, just for a moment," I suggested.

"Why? What is it?"

I shook my head. I didn't know how to answer

him, but I felt something was wrong. Several minutes passed, and nothing happened. Hawk and I both had binoculars trained on the deck of the ship—it was deserted. Hawk still had the radio transmitter in his hand and was growing impatient. I was beginning to doubt my intuition and was about to tell him to give the order to close in when it happened.

We suddenly saw a brilliant burst of orange flame coming from the white ship. It was followed by a deafening explosion. The sleek white vessel blew apart in the sea. It literally disintegrated in a second into a few floating planks. The explosion had been so unexpected and so shocking that almost all of us were briefly frozen into immobility.

Hawk recovered quickly, however, and went into action, shouting orders over the radio transmitter for all the waiting ships to come in and try to pick up possible survivors. At the same time, our launch was bearing down swiftly on the spot where the ship had sunk. But when we and the other ships converged on the area, there was no sign of survivors. In fact, there was nothing at all remaining except for a few charred planks and oil streaks. Still, the search went on well into night, with the waters lit by giant searchlights from the decks of all the vessels. We found nothing.

"It's a mystery to me," Hawk said slowly when the search was finally abandoned and the other ships were waiting for further instructions from him. "Why would they go to all that trouble to collect the two million dollars and then blow up themselves—and the money?"

"That's just it," I said suddenly as I got the idea. "They didn't blow up the money!"

"Didn't blow up the money?" Hawk demanded. "Then where is it?"

"I don't know," I said. "But it didn't go down with the ship. Somehow they managed to get it off before the explosion."

"How? How?" Hawk asked impatiently. "We had it under constant surveillance from the time we first saw it. How could it have been removed?"

"I don't know yet," I admitted. "But they did it. They had always planned to do it this way. They figured that we would have a trap for them after the missile had been returned, but it didn't matter. The money was all that mattered. The rest, the ship, the crew, were to be sacrificed."

"But that's insane," Hawk protested.

"Of course," I told him, "and so is everything else so far."

"Yes," Hawk agreed, speaking slowly, "you're probably right. But how, how, did they manage to remove the money?"

"I don't know yet," I answered again, "but I intend to find out. The answer must be somewhere here along the coast of the Adriatic Sea. I want us to search it, inch by inch, until we find some evidence that there was a survivor, or survivors, who got away with the cash."

Hawk still doubted my opinion, but he agreed to ask the ships standing by to cooperate in helping me look for the evidence. They all offered assistance. Hawk left me at Split because he had to return to the United States to report back to the President personally.

It took us two more days and nights of searching the Adriatic coast before we found the evidence I was sure would be there somewhere. I was notified when a Greek cruiser found it, and rushed to the spot, a lonely stretch of barren land north of Split.

There, washed up on the shore and partly submerged in the sea, was a small, one-man submarine that had been abandoned. But I had my answer of how the two million dollars had been removed from the ship. Probably, soon after we had taken the money aboard in exchange for the missile, it had been turned over to the submariner, and the one-man craft had been dropped from the hold of the ship.

It had been easy for the tiny submarine to sneak out of the harbor, make its way along the coast, and to land. Later, perhaps that same night, or even on one of the following days or nights, the man had probably been picked up by a plane or another boat and had disappeared with the $2,000,000. As soon as I was able to make arrangements over the ship's radio, I put through a call to Hawk, who was back in New York by then. I told him what we had discovered, in code. He took the news more cheerfully than I had expected and instructed me to return to Paris and call him from the AXE office there because he might have some news for me of a new development.

Later that day in Paris, I stopped by the hotel to check in with Elsa before going to the AXE office.

She grabbed me before I got into the door, covered my face with kisses, and said worriedly, "I didn't know what had happened to you, Dumplink. I was about ready to report you to the police as a missing person."

"Business, again," I said. "Sorry I couldn't leave a message. And I have to go out once more. But this time I will be back soon, and maybe we can have some time together."

At the AXE office, Bonaparte put me through to Hawk on a scrambled wire.

"We've got a new lead," Hawk said. "It may be the best one we've had so far. Our research people, who have been running a continuing check on the participants in this case, have finally turned up a definite connection among several of them. You'll remember I mentioned earlier that several of the people had had weight problems. Well, now we've discovered that at least four of them were patients at the same weight-reducing spa in Switzerland."

"That would have to be more than a coincidence," I mused.

"We think so, too," Hawk said. "The place's just outside Berne in the mountains. It's called the Rejuvenation Health Spa and is run by a doctor named Frederick Bosch. What do you think?"

"I think I'd better fly to Switzerland," I said, "and take a look around."

"Yes, I agree," Hawk said. "What will you tell that Von Alder woman, Elsa?"

"I'll tell her I have business in Berne and suggest that she fly back to the States."

"Yes, well," Hawk said, "I have other men watching the rest of the Von Alders. If she comes back, I'll put a man on her, too. I'll be in touch with you when you reach Switzerland."

When I returned to the hotel and knocked on the door of Elsa's suite, I found her having her hair done by the hotel hairdresser.

"I don't like you to see me while I'm trying to get beautiful," she said, frowning from under the hair dryer.

"I had to talk to you," I told her. "I'm going to have to leave today for Berne. My office called, and there's some business there I have to look into."

"Berne!" she exclaimed happily, "but Dumplink, that's marvelous. I'll go with you. There's a simply wonderful health spa outside Berne where Ursie, my sisters, and I often go. We'll fly there in the jet, and I can relax in the spa while you attend to your business."

"What" I asked, "is the name of this spa?"

"It's called the Rejuvenation Health Spa," she answered, as I guess I knew she would. And there, once more, was another link between the Von Alders and the case. I saw no reason why Elsa shouldn't accompany me to Berne, since it might strengthen the link, so I agreed.

After I had phoned Hawk again from my suite and told him that Elsa was going to Berne with me, we checked out of the George V. Then we drove to Orly and boarded the jet, which was still piloted by the two men supplied by the Paris AXE office, for the flight to Switzerland.

Fifteen

The weather was cold and clear when we landed in Berne. Elsa knew of a small chalet on the outskirts of the city, so we took connecting rooms there.

"We always stay at this place," Elsa explained to me after we had settled into our quarters. "It's good to have a spot like this when it becomes too confining at the spa."

I liked our accommodations. It was a clean, quiet, cheerful place, with warming fires burning in every room. The elderly white-haired, apple-cheeked proprietor and his wife had an excellent reputation. From a window in my room, Elsa pointed out the health spa, which was on the top of a mountain some distance away. After she had left me to go to her own room, I studied the spa through my binoculars.

It was a huge sprawling complex, with a multi-storied main building surrounded by several smaller buildings. All were in a dazzling white that blended with the snow-covered peaks jutting up on all sides around it. I could see a twisting

single-lane road that led to the place and a cable
car that was suspended from twin trolley lines
overhead. From that distance, it wasn't possible
to make out much of the details. I wondered how
I would make my approach—secretly, or as a
guest, or, perhaps, through Elsa. But for the time
being, I would bide my time and try to get the
lay of the land. Besides, if the Von Alders were
somehow involved in the plot, Elsa would sooner
or later see to it that I was lured there.

Meanwhile, it probably would be a good idea
to make contact with the local AXE agent. I had
never met him, but Hawk had told me his name
and where to find him. I tapped on the door
that connected my room with Elsa's and told her
I was going out for a while. She would give herself a beauty treatment while I was gone and be
waiting for me when I returned.

Hans Verblen, the local AXE representative,
met me at the door of a modest tailor's shop that
bore his name on one of Berne's side streets.
Verblen was expecting me. He said that Hawk
had already told him the details of my assignment
in a phone call from the States. He was at my
disposal.

"What can I do to help?" the fat dark-haired
man asked.

"Mostly," I told him, "I'd like to have as much
information as you've got on the Rejuvenation

Health Spa. Has there ever been any trouble up there? Who runs it? Information like that."

Verblen nodded, locked the door to his tailor shop, and led me to the basement. It was a spacious, soundproof area with file cabinets solidly lining the wall. There were cameras, tape recorders, teletype machines, weapons of all varieties everywhere.

"This is where I do my real work," Verblen explained with a wave of his hand.

"It's quite a set-up," I remarked.

Verblen crossed over to one of the cabinets. "I'm afraid I don't have a very extensive file on the spa. Until Hawk's phone call, I had had no special request to gather intelligence on the place. What I have is strictly routine, no more than I have on every other establishment in the city. There's been no trouble there, as far as I know. They have a steady flow of guests who come from all over the world—most of them wealthy. I always try to photograph as many of the arrivals and departures as I can with a camera using a telescopic lens. But, naturally, I'm sure I've missed a good many."

He dumped the photographs out on the table, and I was amazed to see that there were thousands of pictures.

"You certainly earn your keep, Verblen," I said, shaking my head at the proof of his thoroughness. I thumbed through a few of the photos and spotted all four of the Von Alders in pictures taken at different times.

"Do you think these will be of any help to you?" Verblen asked.

"Not at the moment, I'm afraid," I told him. "They may come in handy later. What I'm interested in right now is anything you can show me or tell me about the inside of the spa. And about Frederick Bosch, the doctor who runs it."

"There isn't much to show or tell," Verblen answered. I could see he was disappointed in himself. "You understand, that the spa is a very exclusive place. Because there are so many affluent guests, the security is tight. I myself have never been inside, so I have no photographs of the interior. If there had been a special request from AXE, I would have found a way in, of course."

"Yes, I understand, but what about the doctor?"

"Again you will be disappointed in the answer," Verblen said. "I have no photographs of Dr. Bosch because he seldom, if ever, ventures outside. I have heard that he's European. He came here many years ago and opened the spa. At first it was a very modest place, but it was always successful. It has been remodeled frequently over the years to become the imposing structure it is today. I have no dossier on the doctor because he has never been in trouble with any of the Swiss authorities, nor with any other officials as

far as the Interpol files show. I've taken the pre-
caution of checking."

"It's possible that I'll try to slip into the spa
unobserved," I told Verblen. "If I do decide to
try, I might call on you for assistance."

Verblen inclined his head slightly. "Anything
I can do to help, I'm prepared to do. I'm only
sorry that I couldn't provide you with more information."

"You may have assisted me more than you
realize," I said to his surprise. "I've learned from
you, for example, that Dr. Bosch rarely appears
in public. That may not be important, but on the
other hand, it makes me slightly suspicious. Being
suspicious, I'll be more careful."

Verblen led me back upstairs, and I left him
at the door to his shop and started to walk back
to the chalet. The air was crisp and invigorating.
It was late afternoon and most of the shops on
the street were closed and locked. I was enjoying
my walk and preoccupied with looking in the
small shop windows along the street, so I didn't
hear the car when it pulled alongside of me. The
first intimation of danger didn't come until I saw
the reflection in the glass window of one of the
shops of the dark car at the curb near me and
of the five men who had leaped from its open
doors and were now rushing toward me.

I twirled in sudden reflex, my hand going for
Wilhelmina in the shoulder holster, but all five

of them were on top of me before I could pull the Luger free. They came at me from all sides, their fists thudding into my body in short, savage chops. I put up only token resistance—just enough, I hoped, to fool them—and let my body go limp, my head wobble from side to side, and my eyes close in feigned unconsciousness.

"Good," I heard one of the men say, "He's out. Get him into the car. Quickly!"

Two of the men took me by the shoulders and two more grabbed the feet. They began to lug me across the sidewalk. I had let them get me about halfway to the car when I suddenly kicked out with both feet, catching one of the men carrying me by the feet and then the other, full in the face. Both screamed and staggered back, clutching their faces. At the same time I had lunged upward, and as my feet became free, I broke loose from the two men who were holding me by the shoulders. The suddenness of my movements had taken them all by surprise. I turned to run.

The fifth man, who had preceded us to the car, was kneeling by one of the open doors with a gun in his hand. He fired, and the bullet chipped off a piece of pavement about an inch away from me. By then, I had Wilhelmina in my own hand. The man only had the opportunity to snap off one more shot before I had steadied the barrel of my Luger and put a bullet in his belly. He fell backwards into the car, his legs hanging out on the street.

The other four men had darted away to various positions along the street. One ducked into the doorway of a building, two others turned into an alleyway, and the fourth dashed behind a parked car. I was still looking for a place to take refuge. All four opened fire at me at the same time. I fired back and then kneeled and took aim at the exposed legs of the man behind the car. I squeezed Wilhelmina's trigger twice and the man screamed and pitched forward, both legs shot out from under him.

Other shots were coming at me from both sides. I wondered what the peace-loving Swiss citizens were thinking of all the gunfire in their normally quiet town. The gunmen had me pinned down between their own car and the front of the shop where I had been standing when their car had approached. I knew I had to take refuge from the street before they rushed me. But I couldn't run behind the car because they would have a clear shot at me, and the door to the shop behind me was closed and locked.

Then I saw the three gunmen coming for me, and I had to move. I fired off a couple of shots to try to hold them off briefly. There was only one thing possible to do. Lowering my head, with my arms cradled over it to protect my face, I sprinted across the sidewalk and plunged through the glass window of the shop behind me. The glass splintered into great shards that crashed into the street outside, but I was inside and out of immediate danger.

The shop was a small toy store with displays of games and dolls. Apparently it was deserted. I raced on through it and found a back door that opened. I had escaped into a back alley. I ducked around the side of the building just long enough to see the men who had tried to ambush me scurrying for their parked car. Three of them were dragging the other two into the car, and they sped away. By then I could hear the wail of klaxons coming closer. The police were on the way. I headed for my hotel and walked through back alleys until I was well out of the area.

No one paid any attention to me when I entered the chalet. I could still hear the wail of police cars in the distance, and the sound continued for a long time.

As soon as I had reached my room, I grabbed my binoculars and went to the window. I trained the binoculars on the road leading up the mountain to the spa and had no trouble finding the dark car. I had been sure that the men had come from the place, and what I saw confirmed that fact.

Well, I thought, I'd been wanting to go to the spa, all right, but not that way.

The incident had proved that somebody knew

I was interested in the spa and either meant to take me there by force—or see that I never got there alive. How had the five men—who were obviously from the spa—known I was in Berne? Through Elsa—? Perhaps. But I *had* also talked to Verblen, the Swiss AXE agent. Could he have been the one? As I knew only too well from past experience, anything was possible.

Sixteen

"Dumplink," Elsa greeted me as she walked through the door of her room a short while later. "I didn't hear you come back."

I had changed my clothes. As far as she could tell, I looked no worse for wear.

"I just got in a few minutes ago."

"I have the most marvelous surprise for you, Dumplink," she laughed, twirling. She was wearing a pink, ruffled negligee. She turned lightly on her toes, pointed to the open door of her room, and called.

Through the door came the other two Von Alder sisters, followed by their mother, Ursie. Both sisters were wearing pink negligees identical to the one Elsa—or was it Elsa?—was wearing. Ursie had on a quilted housecoat. Looking at the three sisters standing side by side was like looking into three mirrors reflecting the same image.

One of the girls laughed and said, "You were a naughty boy, running away with Elsa. Did you really think you could escape the rest of us that easily? Now you'll pay for that, because we won't tell you which of us is which."

"Since you're all equally beautiful and charming," I replied, "it doesn't matter. My pleasure has increased three-fold."

It was all good-humored and, of course, the kind of thing the Von Alders would delight in doing. But I couldn't help wondering if it was only a prank that had brought them here to Berne, or if it was because I was so close to the spa and they either wanted to find a way to keep me away or a way to get me into the place. Time would tell.

The Von Alders decided that I had to take them to dinner in the diningroom of the chalet, which, they told me, was famous for its excellent cuisine. I agreed, and the four women disappeared through the door, bolting it behind them. I could hear them laughing. Was it because they had tricked me?

Later, when the five of us went down to the diningroom, I discovered what a popular place the chalet was. The diningroom was crowded with guests and the local citizens. Of course, the Von Alders were soon surrounded by men they knew, as almost always happened whenever they appeared in public. Our table of five quickly grew to a table of a dozen or more. I was introduced to each of the new arrivals, most of them members of foreign embassies or such. The Von Alders didn't associate with the common folk.

About midway through the meal, there was a sudden, abrupt break in the chatter and laughter, and every male head in the room, including mine, turned to look at a most beautiful girl who entered and sat alone at a table by the window. She was a striking, willowy redhead in a low-cut gown that clung to her superbly shaped body as if it had been painted on with a brush.

One of the men at our table gave a discreet whistle. "Who is she?"

One of the triplets sniffed and said, "Oh, she's just an employee at the health spa. I've seen her around when we've been there."

The Von Alder women were too experienced to allow male attention to wander away from them for long, and soon I noticed that the men crowded around our table were ignoring the redhead, except for an occasional glance in her direction. I, however, glanced frequently. I thought she would be joined by an escort, but she continued her meal alone.

Just as we finished our dinner, one of the men at our table invited everyone to a large party being given at one of the embassies that evening. The Von Alders were delighted and accepted, and so did the others at the table. I excused myself, saying that I had some work to catch up on and that I would remain at the chalet. Actually, I wanted to do some more thinking about the spa, and I was even considering the possibility of trying to sneak up there. It would certainly be easier for me to work with the Von Alders otherwise occupied. The triplets and their mother were eager to go on to the party, so we said goodnight.

I ordered another cognac. When the waiter brought the liqueur, he handed me a note and pointed to the redhead still sitting alone. I was surprised. In the confusion of the departure of the other guests at our table, I had completely forgotten the girl who had earlier caught my eye.

I opened the note and read, WON'T YOU PLEASE JOIN ME? IT'S URGENT THAT I SPEAK WITH YOU. I wondered why the word URGENT was underlined. I looked over and saw that the girl was watching me gravely, and nodded.

"Mr. Dawes," the girl said in a soft, throaty voice, offering me a slim, shapely hand, "I'm Suzanne Henley." She had an accent that was hard to place—they call it mid-Atlantic, but I detected a very strong British tone. She paused until the waiter had gone and I was seated and then added in an undertone, "Please don't misunderstand, I'm not used to picking up men. But there's an important matter that I must discuss with you." She looked around the diningroom searchingly and then back at me. "We can't discuss it here. I don't know who might be watching. Is there some place we can talk in private?"

"Well, there's my room upstairs," I suggested. "It should be private enough, if it won't bother you."

"I'm sure you're a gentleman, Mr. Dawes," she answered. "Yes, your room will be fine. You go up and after a few minutes I'll follow you."

I told her my room number and stood up to leave. As the waiter came toward the table again to pull my chair back, she offered me her hand and said, "So nice to see you again, and I will give you a call if I'm ever in the States."

I went upstairs to my room, wondering what this latest turn of events could mean. Ten or fifteen minutes passed before there was a light tap on my door. I opened it, and Suzanne Henley stepped quickly inside. I closed and locked the door. She seemed nervous and ill at ease for the first few moments. She prowled the room restlessly, looked out the window, and saw the spa, its lights gleaming in the night.

"Oh, there's where I work," she exclaimed. She spotted the binoculars on the windowsill, picked them up, and focused on the complex of buildings. "You have a very good view of the spa from here," she said as she put the binoculars down and turned toward me again.

"Miss Henley, what's this all about? And won't you please sit down."

She sat in a chair opposite me and thought for a moment before she began. "I don't know what all this means, Mr. Dawes, but I've heard rumors about you up at the spa. And I was worried. I really don't know you, and I don't know what your interest is in the place, but—well, I just didn't feel right about things. I thought I'd tell you, that's all." She paused and shook her head helplessly.

I said as gently as possible, "You realize, Miss Henley, I really don't know what you're trying to tell me."

She took a deep breath and finally settled back in the chair. "I should have explained," she said, "that I've been working at the spa for several years now. I'm a dietician there. But for a while I haven't liked the atmosphere. It feels somehow—well—sinister."

"How do you mean, sinister?" I prodded.

"I don't really know," she said. "Just that there's a lot of whispering and secrecy. And I hear people coming and going in the dead of night. There are security guards all around the place, but the guests don't know it. The guests think they're just employees. But they're very tough-looking men. Day and night I hear whispering, and I picked up your name, Dawes. I guessed there was trouble when five of the security men returned to the spa in a car this afternoon. I just happened to see them. A couple were injured. And I heard your name mentioned again. I phoned around until I located you here. That's why I came here for dinner. I asked the waiter who Mr. Dawes was, and he pointed you out. I just wanted to warn you to stay away."

When I questioned her further, her answers seemed straightforward enough, but I didn't really learn anything that tied into the case, even though we talked for a long while. She could have been on the level, or she could have been a decoy sent to try to discourage me from snooping around.

It was quite late when we finished talking, and she suddenly glanced at her watch and gasped, "Oh, I'm in real trouble now. It's after midnight. Long past curfew for the employees. I can't go back there tonight. They'll demand a detailed explanation of where I've been. I'll have to find a place to stay and slip back in the morning."

She was on her feet, quite agitated, and moving toward the door. She paused in mid-stride and shuddered. "If anyone from the spa should see me out on the streets, they would pick me up and question me."

"That place sounds like a prison."

She nodded her head. "Yes, exactly. That's what I've been trying to tell you."

She had the door open and had started to leave. I grabbed her arm, pulled her back, and shut and locked the door again.

"If it's that dangerous for you," I said, "perhaps

you should spend the night here. You'll be safe."

She looked at me thoughtfully for a long moment, probably considering all the implications of my invitation. I really had no ulterior motive in making the suggestion, except that I wanted to help. But if something else developed. . . .

"You're sure it won't inconvenience you?" she asked.

I shrugged. There were twin beds, as she could plainly see. "You can take one bed," I said, "and I'll just stretch out on the other until morning. You'll be quite safe." I meant it any way she chose to take it.

"All right," she said slowly, nodding her head.

She went into the bathroom. I checked the locks on the doors and turned out the lights in the room. Then I took my shoes off and lay down on one of the beds. It was still bright in the room from the reflection of the moon on the snow outside. She came back in a few minutes, wearing only her slip. As she crossed from the bathroom to the bed, her body was outlined in the light from the window, and I could see that she had nothing else on underneath.

She got into bed and pulled the covers over her. "Good night, Mr. Dawes. And thank you."

"Good night," I said. "Go to sleep now."

For a brief while, I'll admit, the thought of that beautiful body lying so near distracted me from sleep. But she had offered no invitation. I soon drifted off to sleep. I don't think I had slept for very long when I was awakened by soft cries from her bed.

I sat up and leaned toward the bed. "Suzanne? Miss Henley? Are you okay?"

She continued to cry quietly, and I thought that perhaps she was having a nightmare. I moved over and sat on the side of her bed and shook her lightly by the shoulders.

"It's all right," I whispered. "Wake up! It's all right. You're only having a bad dream."

Her arms came up suddenly, encircled my neck, and pulled me to her urgently. Her eyes still shut, she began frantically to cover my face with kisses. "Hold me. Hold me! Love me!"

It was still hard to tell whether she was awake or dreaming, but her hand had moved to my body, fumbling with my pants while she continued to kiss me. I quickly shed my clothing and slid into bed with her.

"Suzanne," I asked again, "are you awake?"

"Love me, please," she repeated. I obliged her.

She responded as if she had prepared for the act of love all her life but had never before had an opportunity to actually practice it. Her hunger was enormous, driving her to one erotic stimulation after another until we were both exhausted by repeated climaxes. Never before had I known a woman who responded so fully with every sense, every nerve, of her being. Again and again, her body thrashing wildly on the bed, she turned her head to stifle her cries so that they wouldn't echo through the whole chalet.

Afterwards, as we lay close, she finally opened her eyes and smiled at me. "At first," she said softly, "I thought I was only dreaming. But it wasn't a dream, and it was much nicer."

"Yes," I agreed. "It was."

As I started to roll away from her, I felt her hand brush the inside of my left thigh. She was wearing a ring on her finger and I felt it scratch my flesh lightly. I barely felt the scratch, but almost immediately a warm, soothing sensation spread through my whole body. My first thought was that it was just the after-effect of our prolonged love-making. The truth hit me a moment later when that feeling changed to one of overwhelming suffocation. It had happened again— I had been drugged. Suzanne Henley had injected some substance into my body from her ring.

I knew this time that it was a potent drug that I would be unable to resist. Darkness closed in rapidly. My brain fled headlong into a black, empty void.

Seventeen

My vision was blurred by a brilliant, blinding, white light that was shining directly into my eyes. I must have been unconscious a long time. I thought I was paralyzed. I couldn't move my arms or legs. Slowly, as my vision cleared, I saw that I was in a stark white room, like a hospital room, and that the blinding light was coming from a fixture set in the ceiling directly above me. I was lying on my back, and my arms and legs were strapped down securely by leather straps.

I opened my mouth and tried to yell at the top of my lungs, but I made only a hoarse croak. Even so, my sound brought four burly men, in white jackets that hospital orderlies wear, close around me. They raised the upper portion of my bed so that I was sitting upright.

From my new position, I could see two other people in the room besides the four "orderlies." One was my companion of the previous night. Suzanne Henley, her red hair flaming, looked beautiful in a white nurse's uniform and low-

heeled white shoes. The other was a white-haired
man, probably in his sixties, who was dressed in
a white smock, white trousers, white shoes, and
white gloves. He was sitting in a wheelchair. I
knew instinctively that I was now inside the Rejuvenation Health Spa and that this man was Dr.
Frederick Bosch.

The doctor rolled his wheelchair closer to my
bed and gave me a thin-lipped, icy smile. Suzanne
Henley gazed at me briefly without expression
and turned away.

"Welcome to our spa," the doctor said, his
voice thick with a German accent, "although I'm
afraid this visit may not improve your health." He
paused and then added, "Mr. Nick Carter."

His recognition of me gave me a start, and I
struggled futilely for a moment against the bonds
that held me tightly.

The doctor gave a wave with his hand. "It's
quite, quite useless to struggle, Mr. Carter. You
are powerless here. Besides, why should you be
anxious to leave when you've wanted to come
here so much?"

He spun around in his wheelchair and ordered
the four white-coated attendants to take me upstairs.

The men quickly rolled me, still strapped to
the bed, across the room to a large elevator that
appeared immediately when one of them pressed
a button. They pushed me into the elevator, and

we were joined by Suzanne Henley and the doctor in his wheelchair. No one spoke as the elevator lifted soundlessly. We rode up what seemed to be several stories before the elevator stopped, the doors opened, and I was taken into a huge, open room.

As I looked around the room, I saw that it was as large as a square city-block and glassed in from floor to ceiling on all four sides. We were on top of the spa, and since that establishment sat on the peak of a towering mountain, there was a view through the glass wall on every side down into deep valleys. It was a breathtaking sight, especially in full daylight with the sun shining on the snow.

But there was an awesome sight within the room—an enormous humming, buzzing computer in the center that occupied most of the space. Lights from the computer flashed and blinked continuously, and the machine made a steady, quiet whirring sound. Otherwise, since the room was obviously soundproofed, it was eerily silent. The doctor made a motion with his hand, and the four men rolled my bed closer to the machine. When I was in place there, one of the men worked a crank at the foot of my bed and I was suddenly sitting upright, still strapped, with my back up and my legs down as if I were in a chair.

The four men returned to the elevator and left us when the doctor signalled with his hand again.

Suzanne Henley stood beside the computer and began to twist and turn dials while the doctor scooted over in his wheelchair so that he was directly in front of me.

"There it is, Mr. Carter," he said with a flourish of his hand, indicating the computer, "the answer that you have been seeking. There is the power behind what you once called the 'Assassination Brigade.' There it is, and you still don't know what it means, do you?"

He was right. I didn't know the meaning of the computer, nor how it had created a world crisis.

"Who are you?" I asked. "What's this all about?"

The doctor spun away from me, and I noticed for the first time that his wheelchair was fully mechanized, apparently operated by controls that he could manipulate without manual effort. He laughed gleefully as he whizzed once around the room. Then he returned to where I sat.

"Let me introduce myself," he said, making a mock bow from the waist. "Introduce myself by my real name, not the one everyone else knows me by, Dr. Frederick Bosch. It is a name that will be familiar to you—I am Dr. Felix Von Alder. I see the raised eyebrows, Mr. Carter. You know my wife and my three lovely daughters. But that is only a minor part of the story."

He paused for a moment and regarded me

quizzically. "Before I tell you my story, Mr. Carter, I want you to understand why I am telling you. You see, you're now in my power—physically, and soon you will be in my power totally—physically and mentally. Nothing can stop that, I assure you, and you will soon see for yourself. But before that time I want you to hear what happened. You, with your past achievements, are a proper audience for the brilliant tale I have to tell. I wanted you here alive for this moment, because you are someone who can truly appreciate what I have succeeded in doing. Otherwise," he spun once more in his chair, "otherwise, my work would be like creating a great masterpiece, like a symphony that no one who appreciated good music ever heard, or like a painting no one ever saw. You understand?"

I nodded. What was the explanation, I thought, of this apparent madness?

Dr. Felix Von Alder sat motionless in his wheelchair for a moment before he leaned toward me to talk.

He had been a brilliant scientist in Germany, working for Adolf Hitler on the control of human behavior. The experiments in the '30s and '40s had only involved animals and had been very crude, using chemical and surgical methods to alter and control the brain.

"I had some success," Von Alder said proudly, "even then. *Der Fuhrer* decorated me repeatedly.

I was ready to move on to humans. Then it was too late—the war ended. There was an Allied raid on Berlin where I was working—" he paused in his story and slipped off his white smock. I saw that his arms, with his white gloves on the hands, were artificial. He moved his shoulders, and both arms fell to the floor. "I lost both arms in the raid."

Soon after that, he continued, the war ended. When the Russians came to Berlin, they searched for him because they knew of his experiments. When they found him, they'd taken him to the U.S.S.R. In the confusion of the times, the Germans had thought he was dead. There was no record of the continuing existence of Dr. Felix Von Alder.

In Moscow, he continued his work, but he'd had more sophisticated electrical processes at his disposal. The Russians had constructed artificial arms and hands for him, and he'd been a brilliant success.

"But the Russians," he added, "never stopped being suspicious of me." He paused again and moved his hips against the seat of the wheelchair. Both legs, which I now saw were artificial, fell to the floor.

"They cut off my legs so I could never escape. They knew I was their enemy. I have always believed in the superiority of the German people. All my work had been to help the German state rule the world—and now that I've perfected my techniques, my dream will come true.

"But to return to the Russians—they had been investigating the history of the Third Reich and they'd discovered my deep, personal devotion to Hitler. But that didn't stop them from wanting to use my scientific knowledge. They believed I was close to a breakthrough in my experiments. So they kept me in isolation; I had nothing but my work."

Von Alder sat in his armchair in front of me, an armless and legless torso. I could see that he was savoring my revulsion and shock as I stared at him. He gave a high, bitter laugh and, using the muscles in his back, sent the wheelchair zig-zagging across the room and back to me again, proving he was far from helpless even now.

Stationary once more, he went on with his story. In Russia, he had finally perfected a theory to successfully control humans, for by that time, two new developments had been introduced in the world—computers and miniature transistors.

"As soon as I discovered these two elements," Von Alder told me, "I knew I had what I needed. The computer, after all, was simply a mechanical brain that could be programmed to do whatever I wanted it to do—a brain outside a body. I knew that if I placed a tiny transistor inside a human brain, I could feed orders from the computer into the transistor. My subject would be under my absolute control."

But he still had a problem: he hadn't known how to place a transistor, even a mirco-dot transistor, inside the human brain. He continued experimenting, never revealing his theory to the Russians.

Then, Chinese scientists began visiting Moscow to exchange information. Von Alder decided to switch sides. The Chinese seemed to know nothing of his political past and he would be assured of better treatment. He made friends with a Chinese physicist and through him got smuggled out of Russia. It had been easy. Von Alder's artificial arms and legs had been removed and he had been fitted into the bottom of a crate of scientific instruments being flown to Peking.

"Once in China," Von Alder went on, "I found the solution. It was amazingly simple. Can you guess?"

Before I could say anything, he answered himself: "Acupuncture."

He raced on breathlessly with his story. Using the ancient Chinese medical art of acupuncture, he could bury a micro-dot transistor in the human brain. The transistor was fed from a computer and Von Alder's control of the human being was complete.

As he had done in Russia, Von Alder kept his discovery secret. When the right opportunity came, he planted a micro-dot transistor in the brain of a drunken official of the Communist party, a high-ranking member of the government. Then he activated the transistor with a previously programmed computer, and the Chinese helped Von Alder escape to Switzerland.

"Unfortunately," Von Alder sighed mockingly, "the poor Chinese was killed while flying back to his homeland."

As soon as he reached Switzerland, Von Alder had contacted his wife. Unknown to him, she had given birth to their daughters soon after the Russians had taken Von Alder away. Ursula continued to keep her husband's identity a secret because of his association with Hitler, but she had supplied him funds to open a health spa. His family did not know of his current experiments and his daughters never suspected that "Dr. Bosch" was their father.

The spa flourished, attracting an international clientele of the wealthy and powerful. Von Alder spent years building his assassination squad, implanting the micro-dot transistor in the brains of carefully selected patients at the clinic. When the doctor was ready, he simply activated his human robots through the computer.

I'd been silent during his long narrative, partially because Von Alder was talking nonstop and partially because his story was too incredible to comment on. He was clearly mad, but he proved very quickly that he was not stupid.

As if reading my mind, he snapped, "You don't believe me. You think you've been listening to the wild ramblings of a crazy old man."

He wheeled over to the huge computer, saying, "Listen to this, Mr. Carter. Listen carefully." He signalled to Suzanne Henley, who pressed a button. Suddenly, the voice of the President of the United States filled the room. He was discussing the upswing of trade with Russia and China. As his voice continued, Von Alder's wild cackle almost drowned it out.

"Not only do the transistors transmit my orders," Von Alder said, "but they also act as receivers. I can hear conversations taking place all over the world. You are now hearing your president speak through a transistor planted in the brain of one of your State Department's highest officials. They are at a Cabinet meeting."

Von Alder signalled to Suzanne, and she pushed a series of buttons. Conversations from Russia, China, England flooded the room, one after another.

Now I knew how Von Alder followed all my actions, beating me to every destination. He must have had transmitters in the brains of Agent Z1 and Verblen, and perhaps others at AXE.

"Nobody can stop me," Von Alder boasted. "I arranged those assassination-suicides so there would be no questions left when I came in with the big kill. When I threaten now, they'll believe me. And do exactly as I wish."

His eyes glittering, the doctor rolled his wheelchair close until our faces were only inches apart. "Now we shall discuss your future, Mr. Carter. While you were unconscious, I placed a transistor in your brain. In a moment my assistant," he nodded toward Suzanne, "will activate it. From then on, you will be totally and completely in my power, obeying the programmed tape that I have placed in the computer."

Von Alder sat for a moment, staring into my face. He obviously relished my helplessness. I realized only too well his power, and I felt the sweat break out on my body.

Von Alder turned away from me and nodded to the girl. I braced myself as I watched her hand reach for a button on the computer. She touched the button. A set of lights flashed and more buzzing came from the machine. I waited tensely, not knowing what to expect. Would I black out? Would I lose all memory of the past? What would happen? Soon the lights stopped flashing.

"The Nick Carter transistor has been activated, Dr. Von Alder," the girl said in a cool voice. "Function is perfect."

I sat stiffly in the chair. I had felt nothing—

my brain was still operating as clearly as before. I didn't know what had happened, but obviously I was not under Von Alder's control. I tried to make a rigid mask of my face so that he wouldn't detect anything.

Von Alder apparently thought the operation had succeeded. He scarcely gave me a second glance as he wheeled excitedly about the room, talking to himself. "I have succeeded! Again as always!"

He made a motion toward Suzanne and said, almost contemptuously, "Release him, please."

The girl quickly came to my bed and began to loosen the straps that held me. I kept my face averted in case she might see something there to warn her, but she barely glanced at me. When I was finally free, she moved back to the computer. I didn't know how to act then, so I simply sat where I was while Von Alder continued to breeze back and forth, rambling on about his plans.

Suddenly, in the midst of his diatribe, he stopped talking and came rushing at me in the wheelchair, the nerves in his face twitching uncontrollably.

At almost the same moment, Suzanne screamed to me, "Look out, Nick! He knows you're not controlled. He knows! He saw your eyes!"

Her warning came just in time. I leaped from where I was sitting as Von Alder's wheelchair came bearing down upon me. I saw then, too late, that there were two muzzles thrust out under the armrests of the wheelchair. One muzzle was spewing a sheet of searing flame, while a jet of blinding gas was emitted from the other. If I had not jumped when I did, I would have been burned to a crisp cinder. Even so, part of my left shoulder and arm were badly burned, and I was half-blinded as I dodged to one side.

Von Alder, in a frenzy, swung the wheelchair around and came at me again, both muzzles spitting out the lethal flame and hissing gas. I ran, twisting and turning across the room, as he propelled the wheelchair at me. I was burned again across the back before I could elude him, for, this time, he had been traveling too fast. I was near exhaustion, but before he could swing the wheelchair around again, I lunged after him.

As he was spinning the chair around, I sprang for his back and hooked an arm around his neck. The wheelchair was still racing forward, carrying me with it. With my free hand, I dug my fingers deep into Von Alder's neck until I reached the nerve I was seeking. I applied pressure and temporarily paralyzed him. Now he couldn't move even a muscle to try to slow his vehicle. Using all my weight, I swung the speeding wheelchair around and aimed it straight at the wall of glass.

The wheelchair raced full speed toward its

target. I hung on, watching the wall come closer and closer until, when the wheelchair crashed through the glass, I dropped to the floor. The chair, with Von Alder's body in it, shattered through the glass and tumbled end-over-end into the valley below.

Suzanne Henley rushed over to me and helped me to my feet. I looked at her. "You saved me, didn't you?"

"Yes," she answered, clinging to me. "I'll explain it later."

The two of us stood wordlessly at the edge of the room, looking down into the deep chasm below. There, hundreds of feet below, lay Von Alder's body on the glacier ice with the smashed wheelchair next to it. From the height, the body looked like a tiny broken doll whose arms and legs had been torn off. Suzanne shuddered, and I pulled her away from the window.

"The computer," she said, suddenly remembering. "I have to shut it down."

She hurried across the room and pushed the buttons. The rows of lights went out, and the buzzing slowed to a low hum. With a final shudder, the machine stopped altogether and stood silent.

Suzanne looked at me. "It's all right now," she said. "The computer's deactivated. None of the transistors will work, and all of Dr. Von Alder's victims will resume their normal identities. In time the micro-dot transistors—including the one in your brain—will simply dissolve."

I nodded. It was over.

Eighteen

After the computer was stopped, I put in a call to Hawk in the States. I gave him a terse, complete account of what had happened. When I finished, he instructed me to stay at the spa. He would make a full report to the President and to representatives of other governments. Then they would all come to Switzerland to witness the final destruction of the computer.

While Suzanne and I waited, she told me her story. She had worked for Von Alder for two years. She was British, had gotten to him through a classified help-wanted ad in a London newspaper. She had been a lab assistant in London and the spa offered something different to do.

She'd been a virtual prisoner from the day she arrived. Escape was impossible. Even on the night she came to my hotel room, if she hadn't knocked me out, somebody with her—one of Von Alder's goons—would have finished the job.

A combination of hate and despair drove her to take that wild gamble at the computer. She hoped, she prayed, that freeing me would help free her.

Within a few hours, Hawk and his group began to arrive. They were incredulous when I related the full details of Von Alder's story. I think if Suzanne hadn't been there to back me up—and if I didn't have such a solid reputation in the field—I'd have been dismissed as a crank. And of course there was also the computer to provide proof.

Acting on the orders of the President, Hawk had the Swiss authorities rope off the giant machine. On the following day, the spa was cleared of people. Then experts were called in to dismantle the computer. All evidence of Dr. Von Alder's scheme to rule the world—the computer and the spa—was destroyed. The doctor's body was flown to Berlin and placed in the Von Alder family plot in the dead of night. Only Ursula was informed of his death, and she requested that her daughters never know of their father's existence after World War II.

The people of Berne were told by the authorities that the spa had to be destroyed because the structure had been found unsafe. Now that the case was closed and everything accounted for, Hawk, Suzanne, and I met at the chalet, where I still had a room, for a farewell drink. Hawk was flying back that night, but he had generously suggested I might like to stay over another day.

"Well, Nick," he said, clinking glasses with me, "We can score another one for AXE." That was the closest Hawk would ever come to giving me a compliment.

Later, after Hawk's plane had left, Suzanne and I lay in bed in my room. We had made love again, and I pulled her close to me and said, "You know, I feel like I could go on for the rest of my life making love to you. A dangerous feeling."

She raised up on one elbow, leaned over me, and smiled softly. "Maybe, Dumplink," she whispered, "that's just what will happen to you. Don't forget, you still have a transistor embedded in your brain, and I know almost as much as Dr. Von Alder did about controlling people. I might just decide to make a small computer and program you so that you'll have to make love to me day and night."

"You think that scares me?" I asked as I kissed her.

Nick Carter in an unbeatable spy
adventure series

Assignment Israel							30p
Berlin ..							30p
The Black Death							25p
The Bright Blue Death							30p
A Bullet For Fidel							30p
Cairo ..							30p
Carnival For Killing							30p
The China Doll							30p
The Chinese Paymaster							30p
The Cobra Kill							30p
Code Name: Werewolf							30p
Danger Key							30p
The Defector ..							30p
The Devil's Cockpit							25p
Double Identity							30p
Dragon Flame							30p
The Executioners							30p
The Filthy Five..							25p
Fourteen Seconds to Hell							25p
Fraulein Spy							25p
Hood of Death							25p
The Human Time Bomb							30p
Ice Bomb Zero							30p
The Inca Death Squad							25p
Istanbul							25p
Jewel of Doom							25p
The Judas Spy							30p
The Living Death							30p
Macao ..							30p
The Mark of Cosa Nostra							30p
The Mind Killers							30p
Moscow							25p
Night of the Avenger							30p
The Omega Terror							30p
Operation Che Guevara							25p
Operation Moon Rocket							30p
Operation Snake							25p
Operation Starvation							25p
Peking/The Tulip Affair							25p
The Red Guard							30p
The Red Rays ..							30p
The Red Rebellion							25p
Rhodesia ..							30p
Safari For Spies							30p
Saigon ..							30p
The Sea Trap ..							30p
Seven Against Greece ..							30p
The Slavemaster							25p
Strike Force Terror							30p
Temple of Fear..							25p
The Thirteenth Spy							30p
Time Clock of Death							30p

Westerns in Tandem editions

War in Tandem editions

The Battle of Britain (Illus.) H. St. George Saunders   25p
Official records from the British and German sides and the recollections of the pilots themselves. The really authentic story.

Assault from Within Georg von Konrat   35p
Six hundred young Germans trained to speak, think, eat, sleep and dream as Russians were infiltrated behind the enemy lines to cause destruction and chaos.

Rage of Battle T. S. Hope   30p
A savage record of blood, carnage and death, as experienced by a sixteen-year-old infantryman.

Barry's Flying Column Ewan Butler   25p
The story of the I.R.A.'s Cork No. 3 Brigade 1919–21.

Operation Mercury M. G. Comeau   30p
An airman in the Battle of Crete – 'a record of heroism, of endurance, and of gaiety in the most daunting circumstances.' *Air Chief Marshal Sir Philip Joubert de la Ferte.*

Marshal Without Glory (Illus.) Ewan Butler and Gordon Young   40p
The life and death of Hermann Goering.

Evil Genius (Illus.) Erich Ebermayer and Hans-Otto Meissner   35p
The life and death of Joseph Goebbels.

Pocket Battleship Theodor Krancke and H. J. Brennecke   35p
The exciting account of the famous German raider, Admiral Scheer, which sank 152,000 tons of Allied shipping.

The Raider Kormoran Captain Theodor Detmers   35p
The exploits of a German 'mystery ship' in World War II.

Name ....

Address ....

Titles required..

....

....

....

....

....

....

....

- - - - - - - - - - - - - - - - -

The publishers hope that you enjoyed this book and invite you to write for the full list of Tandem titles.

If you find any difficulty in obtaining these books from your usual retailer we shall be pleased to supply the titles of your choice upon receipt of your remittance.

Packing and postage charges are as follows:
1 book – 7p per copy, 2-4 books – 5p per copy, 5-8 books – 4p per copy.

WRITE NOW TO:
> Universal-Tandem Publishing Co. Ltd.
> 14 Gloucester Road,
> London SW7 4RD